NON SANZ DROICT.

William Shakespeare

MUCH ADO
ABOUT NOTHING

Edited by David L. Stevenson

The Signet Classic Shakespeare
GENERAL EDITOR: SYLVAN BARNET

*Revised and Updated
Bibliography*

A SIGNET CLASSIC
NEW AMERICAN LIBRARY

New York and Scarborough, Ontario

COPYRIGHT © 1964 BY DAVID L. STEVENSON
COPYRIGHT © 1963 BY SYLVAN BARNET

SIGNET CLASSIC TRADEMARK REG. U.S. PAT. OFF. AND FOREIGN COUNTRIES
REGISTERED TRADEMARK—MARCA REGISTRADA
HECHO EN CHICAGO, U.S.A.

SIGNET, SIGNET CLASSIC, MENTOR, PLUME, MERIDIAN AND NAL
BOOKS are published *in the United States* by
New American Library,
1633 Broadway, New York, New York 10019,
in Canada by New American Library of Canada Limited,
81 Mack Avenue, Scarborough, Ontario M1L 1M8

12   13   14   15   16   17   18   19

PRINTED IN THE UNITED STATES OF AMERICA

Contents

Shakespeare: Prefatory Remarks

Between the record of his baptism in Stratford on 26 April 1564 and the record of his burial in Stratford on 25 April 1616, some forty documents name Shakespeare, and many others name his parents, his children, and his grandchildren. More facts are known about William Shakespeare than about any other playwright of the period except Ben Jonson. The facts should, however, be distinguished from the legends. The latter, inevitably more engaging and better known, tell us that the Stratford boy killed a calf in high style, poached deer and rabbits, and was forced to flee to London, where he held horses outside a playhouse. These traditions are only traditions; they may be true, but no evidence supports them, and it is well to stick to the facts.

Mary Arden, the dramatist's mother, was the daughter of a substantial landowner; about 1557 she married John Shakespeare, who was a glove-maker and trader in various farm commodities. In 1557 John Shakespeare was a member of the Council (the governing body of Stratford), in 1558 a constable of the borough, in 1561 one of the two town chamberlains, in 1565 an alderman (entitling him to the appellation "Mr."), in 1568 high bailiff—the town's highest political office, equivalent to mayor. After 1577, for an unknown reason he drops out of local politics. The birthday of William Shakespeare, the eldest son of this locally prominent man, is unrecorded; but the Stratford parish register records that the infant was baptized on 26 April 1564.

(It is quite possible that he was born on 23 April, but this date has probably been assigned by tradition because it is the date on which, fifty-two years later, he died.) The attendance records of the Stratford grammar school of the period are not extant, but it is reasonable to assume that the son of a local official attended the school and received substantial training in Latin. The masters of the school from Shakespeare's seventh to fifteenth years held Oxford degrees; the Elizabethan curriculum excluded mathematics and the natural sciences but taught a good deal of Latin rhetoric, logic, and literature. On 27 November 1582 a marriage license was issued to Shakespeare and Anne Hathaway, eight years his senior. The couple had a child in May, 1583. Perhaps the marriage was necessary, but perhaps the couple had earlier engaged in a formal "troth plight" which would render their children legitimate even if no further ceremony were performed. In 1585 Anne Hathaway bore Shakespeare twins.

That Shakespeare was born is excellent; that he married and had children is pleasant; but that we know nothing about his departure from Stratford to London, or about the beginning of his theatrical career, is lamentable and must be admitted. We would gladly sacrifice details about his children's baptism for details about his earliest days on the stage. Perhaps the poaching episode is true (but it is first reported almost a century after Shakespeare's death), or perhaps he first left Stratford to be a schoolteacher, as another tradition holds; perhaps he was moved by

> Such wind as scatters young men through the world,
> To seek their fortunes further than at home
> Where small experience grows.

In 1592, thanks to the cantankerousness of Robert Greene, a rival playwright and a pamphleteer, we have our first reference, a snarling one, to Shakespeare as an actor and playwright. Greene warns those of his own educated friends who wrote for the theater against an actor who has presumed to turn playwright:

There is an upstart crow, beautified with our feathers, that with his *tiger's heart wrapped in a player's hide* supposes he is as well able to bombast out a blank verse as the best of you, and being an absolute Johannes-factotum is in his own conceit the only Shake-scene in a country.

The reference to the player, as well as the allusion to Aesop's crow (who strutted in borrowed plumage, as an actor struts in fine words not his own), makes it clear that by this date Shakespeare had both acted and written. That Shakespeare is meant is indicated not only by "Shake-scene" but by the parody of a line from one of Shakespeare's plays, *3 Henry VI*: "O, tiger's heart wrapped in a woman's hide." If Shakespeare in 1592 was prominent enough to be attacked by an envious dramatist, he probably had served an apprenticeship in the theater for at least a few years.

In any case, by 1592 Shakespeare had acted and written, and there are a number of subsequent references to him as an actor: documents indicate that in 1598 he is a "principal comedian," in 1603 a "principal tragedian," in 1608 he is one of the "men players." The profession of actor was not for a gentleman, and it occasionally drew the scorn of university men who resented writing speeches for persons less educated than themselves, but it was respectable enough: players, if prosperous, were in effect members of the bourgeoisie, and there is nothing to suggest that Stratford considered William Shakespeare less than a solid citizen. When, in 1596, the Shakespeares were granted a coat of arms, the grant was made to Shakespeare's father, but probably William Shakespeare (who the next year bought the second-largest house in town) had arranged the matter on his own behalf. In subsequent transactions he is occasionally styled a gentleman.

Although in 1593 and 1594 Shakespeare published two narrative poems dedicated to the Earl of Southampton, *Venus and Adonis* and *The Rape of Lucrece,* and may well have written most or all of his sonnets in the middle nineties, Shakespeare's literary activity seems to have been almost entirely devoted to the theater. (It may be significant that the two narrative poems were written in years when the plague closed the theaters for several months.) In 1594 he was a charter member of a theatrical company called the Chamberlain's Men (which in 1603 changed its name to the King's Men); until he retired to Stratford (about 1611, apparently), he was with this remarkably stable company. From 1599 the company acted primarily at the Globe Theatre, in which Shakespeare held a one-tenth interest. Other Elizabethan dramatists are known to have acted, but no other is known also to have been entitled to a share in the profits of the playhouse.

Shakespeare's first eight published plays did not have his name on them, but this is not remarkable; the most popular play of the sixteenth century, Thomas Kyd's *The Spanish Tragedy,* went through many editions without naming Kyd, and Kyd's authorship is known only because a book on the profession of acting happens to quote (and attribute to Kyd) some lines on the interest of Roman emperors in the drama. What is remarkable is that after 1598 Shakespeare's name commonly appears on printed plays—some of which are not his. Another indication of his popularity comes from Francis Meres, author of *Palladis Tamia: Wit's Treasury* (1598): in this anthology of snippets accompanied by an essay on literature, many playwrights are mentioned, but Shakespeare's name occurs more often than any other, and Shakespeare is the only playwright whose plays are listed.

From his acting, playwriting, and share in a theater, Shakespeare seems to have made considerable money. He put it to work, making substantial investments in Stratford real estate. When he made his will (less than a month before he died), he sought to leave his property intact to his descendants. Of small bequests to relatives and to friends (including three actors, Richard Burbage, John Hemin-ges, and Henry Condell), that to his wife of the second-best bed has provoked the most comment; perhaps it was the bed the couple had slept in, the best being reserved for visitors. In any case, had Shakespeare not excepted it, the bed would have gone (with the rest of his household possessions) to his daughter and her husband. On 25 April 1616 he was buried within the chancel of the church at Stratford. An unattractive monument to his memory,

placed on a wall near the grave, says he died on 23 April.
Over the grave itself are the lines, perhaps by Shakespeare,
that (more than his literary fame) have kept his bones
undisturbed in the crowded burial ground where old bones
were often dislodged to make way for new:

> Good friend, for Jesus' sake forbear
> To dig the dust enclosed here.
> Blessed be the man that spares these stones
> And cursed be he that moves my bones.

Thirty-seven plays, as well as some nondramatic poems,
are held to constitute the Shakespeare canon. The dates
of composition of most of the works are highly uncertain,
but there is often evidence of a *terminus a quo* (starting
point) and/or a *terminus ad quem* (terminal point) that
provides a framework for intelligent guessing. For example, *Richard II* cannot be earlier than 1595, the publication date of some material to which it is indebted; *The
Merchant of Venice* cannot be later than 1598, the year
Francis Meres mentioned it. Sometimes arguments for a
date hang on an alleged topical allusion, such as the lines
about the unseasonable weather in *A Midsummer Night's
Dream,* II.i.81–117, but such an allusion (if indeed it is an
allusion) can be variously interpreted, and in any case
there is always the possibility that a topical allusion was
inserted during a revision, years after the composition of
a play. Dates are often attributed on the basis of style,
and although conjectures about style usually rest on other
conjectures, sooner or later one must rely on one's literary
sense. There is no real proof, for example, that *Othello*
is not as early as *Romeo and Juliet,* but one feels *Othello*
is later, and because the first record of its performance is
1604, one is glad enough to set its composition at that
date and not push it back into Shakespeare's early years.
The following chronology, then, is as much indebted to
informed guesswork and sensitivity as it is to fact. The
dates, necessarily imprecise, indicate something like a
scholarly consensus.

PLAYS

1588–93	The Comedy of Errors
1588–94	Love's Labor's Lost
1590–91	2 Henry VI
1590–91	3 Henry VI
1591–92	1 Henry VI
1592–93	Richard III
1592–94	Titus Andronicus
1593–94	The Taming of the Shrew
1593–95	The Two Gentlemen of Verona
1594–96	Romeo and Juliet
1595	Richard II
1594–96	A Midsummer Night's Dream
1596–97	King John
1596–97	The Merchant of Venice
1597	1 Henry IV
1597–98	2 Henry IV
1598–1600	Much Ado About Nothing
1598–99	Henry V
1599	Julius Caesar
1599–1600	As You Like It
1599–1600	Twelfth Night
1600–01	Hamlet
1597–1601	The Merry Wives of Windsor
1601–02	Troilus and Cressida
1602–04	All's Well That Ends Well
1603–04	Othello
1604	Measure for Measure
1605–06	King Lear
1605–06	Macbeth
1606–07	Antony and Cleopatra
1605–08	Timon of Athens
1607–09	Coriolanus
1608–09	Pericles
1609–10	Cymbeline
1610–11	The Winter's Tale
1611	The Tempest
1612–13	Henry VIII

1592	*Venus and Adonis*
1593–94	*The Rape of Lucrece*
1593–1600	*Sonnets*
1600–01	*The Phoenix and the Turtle*

Shakespeare's Theater

In Shakespeare's infancy, Elizabethan actors performed wherever they could—in great halls, at court, in the court-yards of inns. The innyards must have made rather un-satisfactory theaters: on some days they were unavail-able because carters bringing goods to London used them as depots; when available, they had to be rented from the innkeeper; perhaps most important, London inns were subject to the Common Council of London, which was not well disposed toward theatricals. In 1574 the Com-mon Council required that plays and playing places in London be licensed. It asserted that

> sundry great disorders and inconveniences have been found to ensue to this city by the inordinate haunting of great multitudes of people, specially youth, to plays, inter-ludes, and shows, namely occasion of frays and quarrels, evil practices of incontinency in great inns having cham-bers and secret places adjoining to their open stages and galleries,

and ordered that innkeepers who wished licenses to hold performances put up a bond and make contributions to the poor.

The requirement that plays and innyard theaters be licensed, along with the other drawbacks of playing at inns, probably drove James Burbage (a carpenter-turned-actor) to rent in 1576 a plot of land northeast of the city walls and to build here—on property outside the jurisdic-tion of the city—England's first permanent construction designed for plays. He called it simply the Theatre. About all that is known of its construction is that it was wood.

It soon had imitators, the most famous being the Globe (1599), built across the Thames (again outside the city's jurisdiction), out of timbers of the Theatre, which had been dismantled when Burbage's lease ran out.

There are three important sources of information about the structure of Elizabethan playhouses—drawings, a contract, and stage directions in plays. Of drawings, only the so-called De Witt drawing (c. 1596) of the Swan—really a friend's copy of De Witt's drawing—is of much significance. It shows a building of three tiers, with a stage jutting from a wall into the yard or center of the building. The tiers are roofed, and part of the stage is covered by a roof that projects from the rear and is supported at its front on two posts, but the groundlings, who paid a penny to stand in front of the stage, were exposed to the sky. (Performances in such a playhouse were held only in the daytime; artificial illumination was not used.) At the rear of the stage are two doors; above the stage is a gallery. The second major source of information, the contract for the Fortune, specifies that although the Globe is to be the model, the Fortune is to be square, eighty feet outside and fifty-five inside. The stage is to be forty-three feet broad, and is to extend into the middle of the yard (i.e., it is twenty-seven and a half feet deep). For patrons willing to pay more than the general admission charged of the groundlings, there were to be three galleries provided with seats. From the third chief source, stage directions, one learns that entrance to the stage was by doors, presumably spaced widely apart at the rear ("Enter one citizen at one door, and another at the other"), and that in addition to the platform stage there was occasionally some sort of curtained booth or alcove allowing for "discovery" scenes, and some sort of playing space "aloft" or "above" to represent (for example) the top of a city's walls or a room above the street. Doubtless each theater had its own peculiarities, but perhaps we can talk about a "typical" Elizabethan theater if we realize that no theater need exactly have fit the description, just as no father is the typical father with 3.7 children. This hypothetical theater is wooden, round or polygonal (in *Henry V* Shakespeare calls it a "wooden _O_"), capable of holding some eight hundred spectators standing in the yard around the projecting elevated stage and some fifteen hundred additional spectators seated in the three roofed galleries. The stage, protected by a "shadow" or "heavens" or roof, is entered by two doors; behind the doors is the "tiring house" (attiring house, i.e., dressing room), and above the doors is some sort of gallery that may sometimes hold spectators but that can be used (for example) as the bedroom from which Romeo—according to a stage direction in one text —"goeth down." Some evidence suggests that a throne can be lowered onto the platform stage, perhaps from the "shadow"; certainly characters can descend from the stage through a trap or traps into the cellar or "hell." Sometimes this space beneath the platform accommodates a sound-effects man or musician (in _Antony and Cleopatra_ "music of the hautboys is under the stage") or an actor (in _Hamlet_ the "Ghost cries under the stage"). Most characters simply walk on and off, but because there is no curtain in front of the platform, corpses will have to be carried off (Hamlet must lug Polonius' guts into the neighbor room), or will have to fall at the rear, where the curtain on the alcove or booth can be drawn to conceal them.

Such may have been the so-called "public theater." Another kind of theater, called the "private theater" because its much greater admission charge limited its audience to the wealthy or the prodigal, must be briefly mentioned. The private theater was basically a large room, entirely roofed and therefore artificially illuminated, with a stage at one end. In 1576 one such theater was established in Blackfriars, a Dominican priory in London that had been suppressed in 1538 and confiscated by the Crown and thus was not under the city's jurisdiction. All the actors in the Blackfriars theater were boys about eight to thirteen years old (in the public theaters similar boys played female parts; a boy Lady Macbeth played to a man Macbeth). This private theater had a precarious existence, and ceased operations in 1584. In 1596 James Burbage, who had already made theatrical history by building the Theatre, began to construct a second Blackfriars theater.

He died in 1597, and for several years this second Black-friars theater was used by a troupe of boys, but in 1608 two of Burbage's sons and five other actors (including Shakespeare) became joint operators of the theater, using it in the winter when the open-air Globe was unsuitable. Perhaps such a smaller theater, roofed, artificially illuminated, and with a tradition of a courtly audience, exerted an influence on Shakespeare's late plays.

Performances in the private theaters may well have had intermissions during which music was played, but in the public theaters the action was probably uninterrupted, flowing from scene to scene almost without a break. Actors would enter, speak, exit, and others would immediately enter and establish (if necessary) the new locale by a few properties and by words and gestures. Here are some samples of Shakespeare's scene painting:

> This is Illyria, lady.

> Well, this is the Forest of Arden.

> This castle hath a pleasant seat; the air
> Nimbly and sweetly recommends itself
> Unto our gentle senses.

On the other hand, it is a mistake to conceive of the Elizabethan stage as bare. Although Shakespeare's Chorus in *Henry V* calls the stage an "unworthy scaffold" and urges the spectators to "eke out our performance with your mind," there was considerable spectacle. The last act of *Macbeth,* for example, has five stage directions calling for "drum and colors," and another sort of appeal to the eye is indicated by the stage direction "Enter Macduff, with Macbeth's head." Some scenery and properties may have been substantial; doubtless a throne was used, and in one play of the period we encounter this direction: "Hector takes up a great piece of rock and casts at Ajax, who tears up a young tree by the roots and assails Hector." The matter is of some importance, and will be glanced at again in the next section.

The Texts of Shakespeare

Though eighteen of his plays were published during his
lifetime, Shakespeare seems never to have supervised their
publication. There is nothing unusual here; when a playwright sold a play to a theatrical company he surrendered
his ownership of it. Normally a company would not publish the play, because to publish it meant to allow com-
petitors to acquire the piece. Some plays, however, did
get published: apparently treacherous actors sometimes
pieced together a play for a publisher, sometimes a company in need of money sold a play, and sometimes a company allowed a play to be published that no longer drew
audiences. That Shakespeare did not concern himself with
publication, then, is scarcely remarkable; of his contemporaries only Ben Jonson carefully supervised the publication of his own plays. In 1623, seven years after Shakespeare's death, John Heminges and Henry Condell (two
senior members of Shakespeare's company, who had performed with him for about twenty years) collected his
plays—published and unpublished—into a large volume,
commonly called the First Folio. (A folio is a volume con-
sisting of sheets that have been folded once, each sheet
thus making two leaves, or four pages. The eighteen plays
published during Shakespeare's lifetime had been issued
one play per volume in small books called quartos. Each
sheet in a quarto has been folded twice, making four
leaves, or eight pages.) The First Folio contains thirty-six
plays; a thirty-seventh, *Pericles,* though not in the Folio,
is regarded as canonical. Heminges and Condell suggest
in an address "To the great variety of readers" that the
republished plays are presented in better form than in the
quartos: "Before you were abused with diverse stolen and
surreptitious copies, maimed and deformed by the frauds
and stealths of injurious impostors that exposed them;
even those, are now offered to your view cured and perfect
of their limbs, and all the rest absolute in their numbers,
as he [i.e., Shakespeare] conceived them."

Whoever was assigned to prepare the texts for publication in the First Folio seems to have taken his job seriously

and yet not to have performed it with uniform care. The sources of the texts seem to have been, in general, good unpublished copies or the best published copies. The first play in the collection, *The Tempest,* is divided into acts and scenes, has unusually full stage directions and descriptions of spectacle, and concludes with a list of the characters, but the editor was not able (or willing) to present all of the succeeding texts so fully dressed. Later texts occasionally show signs of carelessness: in one scene of *Much Ado About Nothing* the names of actors, instead of characters, appear as speech prefixes, as they had in the quarto, which the Folio reprints; proofreading throughout the Folio is spotty and apparently was done without reference to the printer's copy; the pagination of *Hamlet* jumps from 156 to 257.

A modern editor of Shakespeare must first select his copy; no problem if the play exists only in the Folio, but a considerable problem if the relationship between a quarto and the Folio—or an early quarto and a later one —is unclear. When an editor has chosen what seems to him to be the most authoritative text or texts for his copy, he has not done with making decisions. First of all, he must reckon with Elizabethan spelling. If he is not producing a facsimile, he probably modernizes it, but ought he to preserve the old form of words that apparently were pronounced quite unlike their modern forms—"lanthorn," "alablaster"? If he preserves these forms, is he really preserving Shakespeare's forms or perhaps those of a compositor in the printing house? What is one to do when one finds "lanthorn" and "lantern" in adjacent lines? (The editors of this series in general, but not invariably, assume that words should be spelled in their modern form.) Elizabethan punctuation, too, presents problems. For example in the First Folio, the only text for the play, Macbeth rejects his wife's idea that he can wash the blood from his hand:

> no: this my Hand will rather
> The multitudinous Seas incarnardine,
> Making the Greene one, Red.

Obviously an editor will remove the superfluous capitals, and he will probably alter the spelling to "incarnadine," but will he leave the comma before "red," letting Macbeth speak of the sea as "the green one," or will he (like most modern editors) remove the comma and thus have Macbeth say that his hand will make the ocean *uniformly* red?

An editor will sometimes have to change more than spelling or punctuation. Macbeth says to his wife:

> I dare do all that may become a man,
> Who dares no more, is none.

For two centuries editors have agreed that the second line is unsatisfactory, and have emended "no" to "do": "Who dares do more is none." But when in the same play Ross says that fearful persons

> floate vpon a wilde and violent Sea
> Each way, and moue,

need "move" be emended to "none," as it often is, on the hunch that the compositor misread the manuscript? The editors of the Signet Classic Shakespeare have restrained themselves from making abundant emendations. In their minds they hear Dr. Johnson on the dangers of emending: "I have adopted the Roman sentiment, that it is more honorable to save a citizen than to kill an enemy." Some departures (in addition to spelling, punctuation, and lineation) from the copy text have of course been made, but the original readings are listed in a note following the play, so that the reader can evaluate them for himself.

The editors of the Signet Classic Shakespeare, following tradition, have added line numbers and in many cases act and scene divisions as well as indications of locale at the beginning of scenes. The Folio divided most of the plays into acts and some into scenes. Early eighteenth-century editors increased the divisions. These divisions, which provide a convenient way of referring to passages in the plays, have been retained, but when not in the text chosen as the basis for the Signet Classic text they are enclosed in square brackets [ ] to indicate that they are editorial additions. Similarly, although no play of Shakespeare's published during his lifetime was equipped with indications of locale at the heads of scene divisions, locales have here been added in square brackets for the convenience of the reader, who lacks the information afforded to spectators by costumes, properties, and gestures. The spectator can tell at a glance he is in the throne room, but without an editorial indication the reader may be puzzled for a while. It should be mentioned, incidentally, that there are a few authentic stage directions—perhaps Shakespeare's, perhaps a prompter's—that suggest locales: for example, "Enter Brutus in his orchard," and "They go up into the Senate house." It is hoped that the bracketed additions provide the reader with the sort of help provided in these two authentic directions, but it is equally hoped that the reader will remember that the stage was not loaded with scenery.

No editor during the course of his work can fail to recollect some words Heminges and Condell prefixed to the Folio:

> It had been a thing, we confess, worthy to have been wished, that the author himself had lived to have set forth and overseen his own writings. But since it hath been ordained otherwise, and he by death departed from that right, we pray you do not envy his friends the office of their care and pain to have collected and published them.

Nor can an editor, after he has done his best, forget Heminges and Condell's final words: "And so we leave you to other of his friends, whom if you need can be your guides. If you need them not, you can lead yourselves, and others. And such readers we wish him."

SYLVAN BARNET
Tufts University

Introduction

Much Ado About Nothing presents an editor with no significant problems as to when it was written, the correctness of the text, the kind of source material that it reanimates and makes into a play. It was published in quarto in 1600, when Shakespeare was thirty-six, with his name on the title page, and was further identified as having been "publicly acted" by the acting company for which he wrote and of which he was a member. The evidence is quite clear that it had been written within a year or a year and a half of its publication (i.e., at about mid-point in Shakespeare's career as a dramatist). The text itself is an excellent one, the basis of the posthumous Folio text of 1623, with only a few minor difficulties as to the assignment of lines and as to the intent, here and there, of the original punctuation. The Hero-Claudio-Don John plot, with its lady's maid, caught with her lover, being mistaken for the lady herself, has been traced back to a Greek source of about the year 400. The sixteenth-century Italian collector of tales, Bandello, used the plot in Story XXII of his *Novelle* (1554), as did Ariosto somewhat earlier in Book V of his *Orlando Furioso*,[1] and as did Spenser in Book II, Canto 4, of *The Faerie Queene* (1590). Beatrice and Benedick, if one wishes to abstract them from the play to view them in historical context, are part of a battle of the sexes with deep roots in the culture and in the literature of the Western world (as I have tried to demonstrate

---

[1] The famous Elizabethan translation (1591) was by the favorite of the Queen, Sir John Harington.

in *The Love-Game Comedy,* 1946). Dogberry and Verges have self-evident origins in that which they parody.

Much Ado, moreover, has never provoked elaborate critical appraisal, perhaps because it has always seemed serenely self-contained, a comedy that does its work so well when seen on a stage, or when read, that it does not particularly invite extended comment. Its brilliance as a comedy, then (to justify the admirable quietness of its critics), can be briefly verbalized in two interrelated ways. We can describe the dramatic strategies employed in the play, which create its idiosyncratic "tone" as a comedy. We can also try to define the unique identity of *Much Ado* by an exploration of its substance, the special aspect of existence blocked out for dramatization in the play.

The primary identifying fact about *Much Ado,* I think, is that it is the most realistic of Shakespeare's love comedies written during the reign of Elizabeth. And it is realistic despite the basic improbability (or conventionality) of Claudio's deception by Don John. It abandons completely the romantic landscape, the romantic disguisings, the romantic dialogue of Portia's and Bassanio's Belmont, of Rosalind's and Orlando's Forest of Arden, of Viola's and Duke Orsino's Illyria. In *Much Ado* we enter a dramatic world created in very close imitation of the habitable one we know outside the theater.

From its very beginning, the play forces this real world upon us. Its characters are a small group of aristocrats who have all known each other a long time and who are introduced to us, in I.i, talking about each other on the basis of old familiarity. Hero, for example, recognizes at once Beatrice's oblique reference to Benedick as "Signior Mountanto." Beatrice, we are to understand, has taunted Benedick's valor sometime before the immediate moments of the play and remembers that she has promised "to eat all of his killing" in the wars that have just concluded. She has also previously ridiculed his pretensions as a lover. She recalls: "He set up his bills here in Messina and challenged Cupid at the flight." Leonato refers easily to the long-standing "merry war betwixt Signior Benedick" and Beatrice. Claudio confesses to earlier amorous thoughts about Hero before he went off to the "rougher task" of the wars. Even Don John (I.iii) has already been sufficiently irritated by the "exquisite" Claudio to abhor the elegance of this "very forward March-chick," this "start-up," and to be "sick in displeasure to him" (II.ii).

Our sense of the close approximation of *Much Ado* to an actual social world is further enhanced by a certain casualness and easiness in the confrontations of one character with another. In this respect, and scene by scene, *Much Ado* is more like *Hamlet,* for example, than it is like *As You Like It* or *Twelfth Night.* The first and the last scene in the play are perhaps the most brilliant illustrations of this casualness, this incredible ease with which characters react to each other. But it is an ease that is completely sustained as "tone" or manner throughout the play. One finds it in Don Pedro's and in Benedick's teasing of Balthasar, for example, for his reluctance to sing in front of them (II.iii). It is the element which gives credibility to Borachio's rambling discourse to Conrade on fashion (III.iii). It is what makes Benedick's sudden playing the role of schoolteacher and grammarian ("How now? Interjections?") in the church scene (IV.i) so believable and so desperately ironic. It is what makes so devastating the unexpected and embarrassed encounter that Don Pedro and Claudio have with Leonato and Antonio after the disgracing of Hero (V.i).

Another aspect of the sustained, mimetic realism of *Much Ado* has to do with the kind of language that makes up the complex, closely interwoven dialogue of the play. The language used to carry the interchanges between Rosalind and Orlando, or between Viola and Duke Orsino, is romantically stylized and tempts us to immerse ourselves in some ideal, golden world of love. The language used for the interchanges between characters in *Much Ado* constantly reminds us of the flow of clever discourse in the best moments of the actual world we all inhabit. And the potency of this language of *Much Ado* is such that it seems capable of generating the natural, this-worldly atmosphere of the play just in itself. It is not the formalized repartee, the carefully contrived and balanced give and take of wit in Restoration comedy. Rather, its special quality is its air of the spontaneous. In *Much Ado* it is as if the characters themselves were inventing in front of us their quick ironic retorts and their exultant gaiety at the accomplishment.

The characters in this play take their dramatic world to be so much alive that they are constantly remembering what they have said to each other earlier in the action. The most striking example of this sort of realism is the acid repetition to Benedick by Don Pedro and by Claudio (V.i and V.iv) of Benedick's extravagant description (I.i) of what may be done to him if he ever falls in love. But Beatrice, who turns the word "stuffed" inside out in her ridicule of Benedick (I.i), later tempts Margaret to use it against her (III.iv): "A maid, and stuffed!" Don Pedro, with Claudio by (V.i), catches his anger at Leonato's importunate language in the deftly sardonic phrase, "we will not wake your patience." Claudio, moments later in the same scene (after he learns that he has been grossly fooled), expresses his genuine contrition to Leonato by slightly varying the same phrase: "I know not how to pray your patience." Even the two members of the watch, who are worried about "one Deformed" in III.iv, find Dogberry carefully remembering in V.i to have Borachio examined "upon that point."

The sustained, conversational quality of the dialogue of *Much Ado,* which accompanies and gives body to the nonchalant casualness of the character confrontations in the play, is perhaps the ultimate essence of the play's mimetic richness. The characters may individualize what they say, but they all speak essentially the same sophisticated-realistic language of their group. In its imagery it is much concerned with the act of sex and with the expected cuckoldry of their society ("he that is less than a man, I am not for him"; "Tush, fear not, man! We'll tip thy horns with gold"). It is also full of the kind of literary reference that would be known to a person of such a society. Hercules, Ate, Europa and Jove, Baucis and Philemon are tossed into the stream of discourse; Kyd's *Spanish Tragedy* and *A Handful of Pleasant Delights* are quoted; Beatrice makes use of current attitudes already exploited in Davies' poem *Orchestra* in her description of marriage as a dance. But beyond all this sort of identifying conversational style is an "aliveness" in what the

characters say to one another. It is this extravagant "aliveness," in combination with the play's other dramatic de-
vices, that gives to *Much Ado* its separate identity of discourse. In no other of Shakespeare's comedies could one
of its characters call another, with such eloquent under-
statement, "my Lady Tongue."

The substance of *Much Ado* is that of the romantic
comedies, sex, love, and marriage. But this play's differ-
entiated way of regarding this substance, its sophisticated
realism, is certainly intentionally suggested by its title.
Within the play itself there are two views of this substance.
One view is that assumed by Claudio, Don Pedro, Leonato, and Hero. Claudio is the central, dominating voice
of this group as he acts out its social assumptions. He is
presented as a conventional young man, one who regards
love and marriage as the making of a sensible match with
a virtuous and attractive young girl who brings a good
dowry and the approval of her father and of his friends.
Although a young man today, a member of a similar social group, might put his feelings in somewhat more romantic terms, if he were of a "good" family in any city
of the Western world, he might essentially agree with
Claudio's view.

Claudio is certainly no passionate Romeo, and there
is no indication in the play that he has done more than
regard Hero as an attractive member of the aristocratic
society to which they both belong. He is (perhaps somewhat in the position of Paris, in *Romeo and Juliet*) a
young man capable of an easy romanticizing of sexual
attraction, as his comment on Hero to Don Pedro fully
reveals:

> . . . now I am returned and that war-thoughts
> Have left their places vacant, in their rooms
> Come thronging soft and delicate desires,
> All prompting me how fair young Hero is,
> Saying I liked her ere I went to wars. (I.i.291–95)

Claudio, again like Paris, is the young man bent on
doing "the right thing" in his society. He is attractive as
a man, as his worst enemy, Don John, lets us know by
his envy. But Claudio is also, as people aware only of the

right thing to do tend to be, terrifyingly naïve (and terrifyingly obtuse). As Benedick puts it, Claudio reacts like
a hurt bird when he thinks Don Pedro has taken Hero
from him ("Alas, poor hurt fowl! Now will he creep into
sedges," II.i.200–01). And Benedick places Claudio's romantic inclinations toward Hero at the level of the feelings
of a small child by comparing Claudio to a "schoolboy
who, being overjoyed with finding a bird's nest, shows it
his companion, and he [Don Pedro] steals it" (II.i.220–22).
Claudio's politeness, his sense of the socially appropriate,
even leads him to suggest that he abandon his bride immediately after his marriage and accompany his sponsor,
Don Pedro, from Messina to Aragon. Don Pedro again
identifies for us the childlike quality of Claudio's feelings
for Hero when he replies: "that would be as great a soil
in the new gloss of your marriage as to show a child his
new coat and forbid him to wear it" (III.ii.5–7).

In the church scene, Claudio's turning on Hero for her
supposed assignation on the eve of her marriage is wholly
in keeping with the nature of his feelings for her and with
the codes of his group. He moves toward his denunciation
in the sententiously arrogant, teasing manner of the overly
conventional person who has been fooled about something
rather important and who will now take great pleasure
in a measured retaliation. Claudio, the exquisite, reacts
appropriately like a child cheated over a toy promised to
him. And the absolute "rightness" of his attitude in the
play is made quite clear by the fact that Hero's father
and Don Pedro instantly agree with it. Leonato, who was
as concerned as Claudio and Don Pedro with a "good"
marriage, reacts, indeed, much as Capulet (also a socially
conventional man) had reacted when Juliet had refused
to marry Paris:

> Why had I one?
> Why ever wast thou lovely in my eyes?
> . . . mine that I was proud on, mine so much
> That I myself was to myself not mine,
> Valuing of her—why she, O she is fall'n
> Into a pit of ink.   (IV.i.128–39)

Beatrice and Benedick, wholly unchildlike, present another view of the essential stuff of this play, a view that

cuts across the conventional one, and insinuates doubts lurking in sophisticated minds as to its necessary validity. They are everywhere presented as completely aware of the fact that they are playing roles with and for each other —Beatrice as shrew, Benedick as misogynist—and enjoying the playing. The subject matter of their game is a distaste for institutionalized romantic love leading to marriage, the precise kind of "love" that Claudio and Hero accept easily and without thought. The only obstacle to Claudio's pursuit would be the sort of thing he thinks has happened, a lack of sexual virtue on the part of the girl who has caught his fancy. The subtle obstacle to the union of Benedick and Beatrice is that neither is ever sure of what he or she would be like if they agreed to quit playing their respective roles. Indeed, part of the dramatic (and psychological) excitement at the play's end is that neither one of this pair is yet certain of what emotions really lie below the level of the role-playing.

The love game of Beatrice and Benedick is an intricate one in *Much Ado,* because both of them are teasing something more complicated than just conventional romantic love. They are dramatized as testing the antiromantic roles they are actually playing against their sense of what it would be like to be a Hero or a Claudio, to fall into the words and phrases and stances of institutionalized romance. Moreover, in their dueling in the self-accepted roles of the man and the woman too knowing to wear the yoke of marriage and to "sigh away Sundays," it is always made dramatically obvious that both characters are aware that with any slipping either or both could easily *become* a Hero or a Claudio and turn husband and wife. Benedick's first direct comment on Beatrice, early in the play (I.i.184–86), is, it seems to me, self-evident acknowledgment of this fact: "and she were not possessed with a fury, [Beatrice] exceeds [Hero] as much in beauty as the first of May doth the last of December."

It is this ambivalent element in their love game, I think, that made Beatrice and Benedick so fascinating to their own age, and now also to us. And the basis of the fascination is that in their own probing of their reactions to ritualized romantic love, they invite us to probe the usually inaccessible areas of our own knowing, our own awareness in such matters. More important, if we think, at the play's end, that Beatrice and Benedick merely exist for five acts to be tricked into admitting that they are fundamentally as conventionally involved in sex, love, and marriage as Hero and Claudio, we have missed the essential purport of the play.

Beatrice is the more open of the two in her acknowledgment of the ambiguity of her role-playing. Her acid remarks in the first scene of Act I concerning Benedick's challenge to Cupid, and her uncle's fool's response (i.e., Beatrice herself?), carry the suggestion, never made overt in the play, either that Beatrice had never been sure of her role as Lady Tongue or that she had once tried out a romantic role with Benedick himself. She is presented as openly uneasy (II.i) over the fact that Hero has got herself a husband ("I may sit in a corner and cry 'Heigh-ho for a husband!' "). And she once darkly hints an earlier involvement with Benedick when she tells Don Pedro that Benedick lent his heart to her for a while, "and I gave him use for it, a double heart for his single one. Marry, once before he won it of me with false dice" (II.i.275–78).

The ambiguousness in Benedick's role as misogynic bachelor is perhaps best suggested by the extravagant language he always uses to defend his role:

> Prove that ever I lose more blood with love than I will get again with drinking, pick out mine eyes with a ballad maker's pen and hang me up at the door of a brothel house for the sign of blind Cupid.   (I.i.241–45)

His taunt to Claudio concerning Hero ("Would you buy her, that you inquire after her?" I.i.173–74), and his headlong flight from Beatrice (II.i) with the bitter comment that "while she is here" he could live as quietly in hell, are but further illustrations of this extravagance. Dramatically, to be sure, such soaring flights of words prepare us for the irony of his surrender to love of a sort. Psychologically, they tempt us to wonder that a man could hate so vehemently what he professes to have no interest in.

The marriage of Hero and Claudio turns on the simple problem as to whether Hero is a virgin or not, i.e., as to whether she is socially and therefore personally acceptable to Claudio in his aristocratic world of arranged marriages. The marriage of Beatrice and Benedick turns on the ability of their peers to trick them out of their self-conscious role-playing. It is of interest to note that the latter pair's willingness to surrender to love and marriage takes place while Hero's virtue is still under a cloud as far as Claudio is concerned, and therefore at a moment when their previous bantering would be inappropriate. It is equally important to note that both Beatrice and Benedick, if somewhat subdued, actually bring alive again, at the play's end, something of the ambiguity toward love that they had had from the beginning of the play.

Beatrice's final words are not those of a Rosalind or a Viola:

> I yield upon great persuasion, and partly to save your
> life, for I was told you were in a consumption.
>
> (V.iv.95–96)

Benedick's penultimate comments are addressed not to Beatrice, but rather to Don Pedro. And Benedick insists upon being as ambiguous about his feelings, now that he has agreed to conform to marriage, as he had been earlier, when he could only exclaim against it. He insists to Don Pedro that "since I do purpose to marry, I will think nothing to any purpose that the world can say against it" (V.iv.104–06). He concludes that Don Pedro himself had better marry in order that he too may join the gay company of cuckolds-to-be:

> get thee a wife, get thee a wife! There is no staff more
> reverend than one tipped with horn.   (V.iv.122–24)

In *Romeo and Juliet,* written about four years before *Much Ado,* Shakespeare had dramatized the lyric, fragile love of very young people not yet wise enough to yield to the social realities—and therefore broken by them. He had presented their love as a highly perishable commodity, one as subject to accident as to time. It is not only Romeo and Juliet, but we, as audience, who acquiesce in their deaths because we are fully aware that in "reality" there can only be either slow dilution or abrupt extinction of such flowerlike love. In *Twelfth Night,* written probably a year or so later than *Much Ado,* we are kept within the elegant, golden confines of courtly, aristocratic romance —a place full of music and of bodily forms (to borrow from Yeats) "of hammered gold and gold enameling," set singing to keep some "drowsy Emperor awake."

The kind of love encompassed by the dialogue of *Much Ado,* and by its two sets of lovers, is love in the social world. This comedy, indeed, is a highly novel one for Shakespeare to have written. The play ends with its characters and the audience accepting the two marriages that have been in the making from its beginning. But the power of the comedy lies not in our accepting the fragility of youthful passion or in our surrender to idyllic romance. Rather, *Much Ado,* by all its strategies of language and characterization, moves so close to reality that it cannot reach a denouement in which the simply understood mood or attitude of *Romeo and Juliet* or of *Twelfth Night* reaches final focus.

The essential uniqueness of *Much Ado* as a comedy, and its fascination, lies in the fact that it invokes our awareness of the complicated relationship between the indeterminate nature of private feeling and the simplicities of the decorous behavior which is supposed to embody such feeling. That is to say, *Much Ado* dramatizes sex, love, and marriage in close imitation of their complexity in actuality. This play, of course, is far too stylized to be "real," and it keeps us comically insulated from too deep involvement with its characters and its substance. The play's final moment of balance, of standing still, then, is necessarily somewhat different from that of the Shakespearean romances where a long ritual of wooing comes to a ritualized conclusion. In *Much Ado* we are given, in its last scene, the dramatic illusion that the pair of marriages has been created by the volition of the characters themselves. They seem to be marrying out of their own desire to find, if only momentarily, a way of being at peace with themselves and with each other.

DAVID L. STEVENSON
Hunter College

Much Ado About Nothing

Much Ado About Nothing

[ACT I

Scene I. *Before Leonato's house.*]

Enter Leonato, Governor of Messina, Hero his daughter, and Beatrice his niece, with a Messenger.

Leonato. I learn in this letter that Don Pedro of Aragon comes this night to Messina.

Messenger. He is very near by this. He was not three leagues off when I left him.

Leonato. How many gentlemen°[1] have you lost in this action? 5

Messenger. But few of any sort,° and none of name.°

Leonato. A victory is twice itself when the achiever brings home full numbers. I find here that Don Pedro hath bestowed much honor on a young Florentine ·called Claudio. 10

---

[1] The degree sign (°) indicates a footnote, which is keyed to the text by line number. Text references are printed in *italic* type; the annotation follows in roman type.
I.i.5 *gentlemen* men of upper class   **7** *sort* rank   **7** *name* distinguished family

Messenger. Much deserved on his part, and equally rememb'red by Don Pedro. He hath borne himself
beyond the promise of his age, doing, in the figure
15   of a lamb, the feats of a lion. He hath indeed better
bett'red expectation° than you must expect of me to
tell you how.

Leonato. He hath an uncle° here in Messina will be
very much glad of it.

20 *Messenger.* I have already delivered him letters, and
there appears much joy in him; even so much that
joy could not show itself modest enough without a
badge° of bitterness.

Leonato. Did he break out into tears?

25 *Messenger.* In great measure.

Leonato. A kind overflow of kindness.° There are no
faces truer than those that are so washed. How much
better is it to weep at joy than to joy at weeping!

Beatrice. I pray you, is Signior Mountanto° returned
30   from the wars or no?

Messenger. I know none of that name, lady. There was
none such in the army of any sort.

Leonato. What is he that you ask for, niece?

Hero. My cousin means Signior Benedick of Padua.

35 *Messenger.* O, he's returned, and as pleasant° as ever
he was.

Beatrice. He set up his bills° here in Messina and challenged Cupid at the flight;° and my uncle's fool,
reading the challenge, subscribed° for Cupid and
40   challenged him at the burbolt.° I pray you, how
many hath he killed and eaten in these wars? But

15–16 *better bett'red expectation* greatly exceeded anticipated valor
18 *uncle* (does not appear in the play)   23 *badge* emblem   26 *kind
overflow of kindness* natural overflow of tenderness   29 *Mountanto*
a fencing thrust   35 *pleasant* lively   37 *bills* advertising placards
38 *flight* shooting contest (i.e., he thought himself a lady-killer)
39 *subscribed* signed up   40 *burbolt* blunt arrow

how many hath he killed? For indeed, I promised
to eat all of his killing.

Leonato. Faith, niece, you tax° Signior Benedick too
much; but he'll be meet° with you, I doubt it not.   45

Messenger. He hath done good service, lady, in these
wars.

Beatrice. You had musty victual, and he hath holp to
eat it. He is a very valiant trencherman;° he hath
an excellent stomach.   50

Messenger. And a good soldier too, lady.

Beatrice. And a good soldier to° a lady. But what is he
to a lord?

Messenger. A lord to a lord, a man to a man; stuffed
with all honorable virtues.   55

Beatrice. It is so, indeed; he is no less than a stuffed
man.° But for the stuffing—well, we are all mortal.

Leonato. You must not, sir, mistake my niece. There
is a kind of merry war betwixt Signior Benedick and
her. They never meet but there's a skirmish of wit   60
between them.

Beatrice. Alas, he gets nothing by that! In our last conflict four of his five wits° went halting° off, and now
is the whole man governed with one; so that if he
have wit enough to keep himself warm, let him bear   65
it for a difference between himself and his horse. For
it is all the wealth that he hath left to be known a
reasonable creature. Who is his companion now?
He hath every month a new sworn brother.

Messenger. Is't possible?   70

Beatrice. Very easily possible. He wears his faith but
as the fashion of his hat; it ever changes with the
next block.°

---

44 *tax* i.e., tease too hard   45 *meet* even   49 *trencherman* eater
52 *to* in comparison with   56–57 *stuffed man* dummy   63 *five wits*
common sense, imagination, fancy, estimation, memory   63 *halting*
limping   73 *next block* most recent shape

Messenger. I see, lady, the gentleman is not in your
75   books.°

Beatrice. No. And° he were, I would burn my study.
  But I pray you, who is his companion? Is there no
  young squarer° now that will make a voyage with
  him to the devil?

80 *Messenger.* He is most in the company of the right
  noble Claudio.

Beatrice. O Lord, he will hang upon him like a disease.
  He is sooner caught than the pestilence, and the
  taker runs presently° mad. God help the noble
85   Claudio if he have caught the Benedict;° it will cost
  him a thousand pound ere 'a° be cured.

Messenger. I will hold friends with you, lady.

Beatrice. Do, good friend.

Leonato. You will never run mad,° niece.

90 *Beatrice.* No, not till a hot January.

Messenger. Don Pedro is approached.

  *Enter Don Pedro, Claudio, Benedick, Balthasar, and
    John the Bastard.*

Don Pedro. Good Signior Leonato, are you come to
  meet your trouble? The fashion of the world is to
  avoid cost, and you encounter it.

95 *Leonato.* Never came trouble to my house in the like-
  ness of your Grace; for trouble being gone, comfort
  should remain. But when you depart from me, sorrow abides, and happiness takes his leave.

Don Pedro. You embrace your charge° too willingly.
100   I think this is your daughter.

Leonato. Her mother hath many times told me so.

---

75 *books* favor   76 *And* if   78 *squarer* brawler   84 *presently* immediately (the usual sense in Shakespeare)   85 *Benedict* (the
change in spelling suggests a disease based on Benedick's name)
86 *'a* he   89 *run mad* catch the Benedict   99 *charge* burden (of
my visit)

Benedick. Were you in doubt, sir, that you asked her?

Leonato. Signior Benedick, no; for then were you a
child.

Don Pedro. You have it full, Benedick. We may guess   105
by this what you are, being a man. Truly the lady
fathers herself.° Be happy, lady, for you are like an
honorable father.

Benedick. If Signior Leonato be her father, she would
not have his head° on her shoulders for all Messina,   110
as like him as she is.

Beatrice. I wonder that you will still° be talking, Signior Benedick; nobody marks you.

Benedick. What, my dear Lady Disdain! Are you yet
living?   115

Beatrice. Is it possible Disdain should die while she
hath such meet food to feed it as Signior Benedick?
Courtesy itself must convert to Disdain if you come
in her presence.

Benedick. Then is courtesy a turncoat. But it is certain   120
I am loved of all ladies,° only you excepted; and I
would I could find in my heart that I had not a hard
heart; for truly I love none.

Beatrice. A dear happiness to women! They would else
have been troubled with a pernicious suitor. I thank   125
God and my cold blood, I am of your humor for
that.° I had rather hear my dog bark at a crow than
a man swear he loves me.

Benedick. God keep your ladyship still in that mind,
so some gentleman or other shall scape a predesti-   130
nate scratched face.

Beatrice. Scratching could not make it worse and
'twere such a face as yours were.

107 *fathers herself* shows who her father is by resembling him
110 *his head* white-haired and bearded (?)   112 *still* always (the
usual sense in Shakespeare)   121 *loved of all ladies* (he had "challenged Cupid")   126–27 *of your humor for that* in agreement on
that

Benedick. Well, you are a rare parrot-teacher.°

135 *Beatrice.* A bird of my tongue is better than a beast of yours.

Benedick. I would my horse had the speed of your tongue, and so good a continuer.° But keep your way, a God's name! I have done.

140 *Beatrice.* You always end with a jade's trick.° I know you of old.

Don Pedro. That is the sum of all,° Leonato. Signior Claudio and Signior Benedick, my dear friend Leonato hath invited you all. I tell him we shall stay 145 here, at the least a month, and he heartily prays some occasion may detain us longer. I dare swear he is no hypocrite, but prays from his heart.

Leonato. If you swear, my lord, you shall not be forsworn. [*To Don John*] Let me bid you welcome, my 150 lord; being reconciled to the Prince your brother, I owe you all duty.

Don John. I thank you. I am not of many words, but I thank you.

Leonato. Please it your Grace lead on?

155 *Don Pedro.* Your hand, Leonato. We will go together.
          Exeunt. Manent° *Benedick and Claudio.*

Claudio. Benedick, didst thou note the daughter of Signior Leonato?

Benedick. I noted° her not, but I looked on her.

Claudio. Is she not a modest young lady?

160 *Benedick.* Do you question me as an honest man should do, for my simple true judgment? Or would

134 *parrot-teacher* i.e., monotonous speaker of nonsense   138 *continuer* staying power   140 *jade's trick* trick of a vicious horse (i.e., a sudden stop?)   142 *the sum of all* the end of the sparring match   155 s.d. *Manent* remain (Latin)   158 *noted* (1) scrutinized (2) set to music (3) stigmatized

you have me speak after my custom, as being a professed tyrant to their sex?

Claudio. No, I pray thee speak in sober judgment.

Benedick. Why, i' faith, methinks she's too low for a   165
high praise, too brown for a fair praise, and too little
for a great praise. Only this commendation I can
afford her, that were she other than she is, she were
unhandsome, and being no other but as she is, I
do not like her.   170

Claudio. Thou thinkest I am in sport. I pray thee tell
me truly how thou lik'st her.

Benedick. Would you buy her, that you inquire after
her?

Claudio. Can the world buy such a jewel?   175

Benedick. Yea, and a case to put it into. But speak you
this with a sad brow?° Or do you play the flouting
Jack, to tell us Cupid is a good hare-finder and
Vulcan a rare carpenter?° Come, in what key shall
a man take you to go in the song?   180

Claudio. In mine eye she is the sweetest lady that ever
I looked on.

Benedick. I can see yet without spectacles, and I see no
such matter. There's her cousin, and she were not
possessed with a fury, exceeds her as much in beauty   185
as the first of May doth the last of December. But I
hope you have no intent to turn husband, have you?

Claudio. I would scarce trust myself, though I had
sworn the contrary, if Hero would be my wife.

Benedick. Is't come to this? In faith, hath not the world   190
one man but he will wear his cap with suspicion?°

177 *with a sad brow* seriously   178–79 *to tell us . . . carpenter* i.e.,
to mock us with nonsense (Cupid was blind, Vulcan was a black-
smith)   191 *but he . . . suspicion* who (because he is unmarried)
will not fear that he has a cuckold's horns

Shall I never see a bachelor of threescore again? Go
to, i' faith! And thou wilt needs thrust thy neck into
a yoke, wear the print of it and sigh away Sundays.°
195 Look! Don Pedro is returned to seek you.

Enter Don Pedro.

Don Pedro. What secret hath held you here, that you
followed not to Leonato's?

Benedick. I would your Grace would constrain me to
tell.

200 *Don Pedro.* I charge thee on thy allegiance.°

Benedick. You hear, Count Claudio; I can be secret as
a dumb man. I would have you think so. But, on my
allegiance—mark you this—on my allegiance! He is
in love. With who? Now that is your Grace's part.
205 Mark how short his answer is—with Hero, Leonato's short daughter.

Claudio. If this were so, so were it utt'red.

Benedick. Like the old tale, my lord: "It is not so, nor
'twas not so, but indeed, God forbid it should be so!"

210 *Claudio.* If my passion change not shortly, God forbid
it should be otherwise.

Don Pedro. Amen, if you love her, for the lady is very
well worthy.

Claudio. You speak this to fetch me in, my lord.

215 *Don Pedro.* By my troth, I speak my thought.

Claudio. And, in faith, my lord, I spoke mine.

Benedick. And, by my two faiths and troths, my lord,
I spoke mine.

Claudio. That I love her, I feel.

220 *Don Pedro.* That she is worthy, I know.

193–94 *thrust thy neck . . . Sundays* i.e., enjoy the tiresome bondage
of marriage   200 *allegiance* solemn obligation to a prince

Benedick. That I neither feel how she should be loved, nor know how she should be worthy, is the opinion that fire cannot melt out of me. I will die in it at the stake.

Don Pedro. Thou wast ever an obstinate heretic in the despite of° beauty.   225

Claudio. And never could maintain his part but in the force of his will.°

Benedick. That a woman conceived me, I thank her; that she brought me up, I likewise give her most humble thanks. But that I will have a rechate° winded in my forehead, or hang my bugle in an invisible baldrick,° all women shall pardon me. Because I will not do them the wrong to mistrust any, I do myself the right to trust none; and the fine° is (for the which I may go the finer), I will live a bachelor.   230 ... 235

Don Pedro. I shall see thee, ere I die, look pale with love.

Benedick. With anger, with sickness, or with hunger, my lord, not with love. Prove that ever I lose more blood with love than I will get again with drinking, pick out mine eyes with a ballad maker's pen and hang me up at the door of a brothel house for the sign of blind Cupid.   240 ... 245

Don Pedro. Well, if ever thou dost fall from this faith, thou wilt prove a notable argument.°

Benedick. If I do, hang me in a bottle° like a cat and shoot at me; and he that hits me, let him be clapped on the shoulder and called Adam.°   250

Don Pedro. Well, as time shall try:

225–26 *in the despite of* in contempt of   228 *will* sexual appetite
231 *rechate* recheate, notes on a hunting horn   233 *baldrick* belt,
sling (the reference here, and in *rechate,* is to the horns of a cuckold)
235 *fine* finis, result   247 *notable argument* famous example   248
bottle basket   250 *Adam* i.e., Adam Bell, one of the three superlative
archers in the ballad "Adam Bell"

"In time the savage bull doth bear the yoke."

Benedick. The savage bull may, but if ever the sensible
Benedick bear it, pluck off the bull's horns and set
255 them in my forehead, and let me be vilely painted,
and in such great letters as they write "Here is good
horse to hire," let them signify under my sign "Here
you may see Benedick the married man."

Claudio. If this should ever happen, thou wouldst be
260 horn-mad.°

Don Pedro. Nay, if Cupid have not spent all his quiver
in Venice,° thou wilt quake for this shortly.

Benedick. I look for an earthquake too then.

Don Pedro. Well, you will temporize with the hours.°
265 In the meantime, good Signior Benedick, repair to
Leonato's. Commend me to him and tell him I will
not fail him at supper; for indeed he hath made
great preparation.

Benedick. I have almost matter° enough in me for
270 such an embassage, and so I commit you—

Claudio. To the tuition° of God. From my house, if
I had it—

Don Pedro. The sixth of July. Your loving friend,
Benedick.

275 *Benedick.* Nay, mock not, mock not. The body of your
discourse is sometime guarded° with fragments,
and the guards are but slightly basted on neither.
Ere you flout old ends° any further, examine your
conscience. And so I leave you.   *Exit.*

Claudio. My liege, your Highness now may do me
280 good.

---

260 *horn-mad* mad with jealousy (perhaps also "sexually insatia-
ble") 262 *Venice* (famous for sexual license) 264 *temporize
with the hours* change temper or attitude with time 269 *matter*
sense 271 *tuition* custody 276 *guarded* trimmed (used of cloth-
ing) 278 *flout old ends* i.e., indulge in derision at my expense

Don Pedro. My love is thine to teach. Teach it but
  how,
  And thou shalt see how apt it is to learn
  Any hard lesson that may do thee good.

Claudio. Hath Leonato any son, my lord?

Don Pedro. No child but Hero; she's his only heir.   285
  Dost thou affect° her, Claudio?

Claudio.   O my lord,
  When you went onward on this ended action,°
  I looked upon her with a soldier's eye,
  That liked, but had a rougher task in hand
  Than to drive liking to the name of love.   290
  But now I am returned and that° war-thoughts
  Have left their places vacant, in their rooms
  Come thronging soft and delicate desires,
  All prompting me how fair young Hero is,
  Saying I liked her ere I went to wars.   295

Don Pedro. Thou wilt be like a lover presently
  And tire the hearer with a book of words.
  If thou dost love fair Hero, cherish it,
  And I will break° with her and with her father,
  And thou shalt have her. Was't not to this end   300
  That thou began'st to twist so fine a story?

Claudio. How sweetly you do minister to love,
  That know love's grief by his complexion!°
  But lest my liking might too sudden seem,
  I would have salved it with a longer treatise.   305

Don Pedro. What need the bridge much broader than
    the flood?
  The fairest grant is the necessity.°
  Look, what will serve is fit. 'Tis once,° thou lovest,
  And I will fit thee with the remedy.
  I know we shall have reveling tonight.   310

---

286 *affect* love   287 *ended action* war just concluded   291 *that*
because   299 *break* open negotiations   303 *complexion* appearance
307 *The fairest grant is the necessity* the most attractive giving is
when the receiver really needs something   308 *'Tis once* in short

I will assume thy part in some disguise
And tell fair Hero I am Claudio,
And in her bosom I'll unclasp my heart
And take her hearing prisoner with the force
315 And strong encounter of my amorous tale;
Then after to her father will I break,
And the conclusion is, she shall be thine.
In practice let us put it presently.   *Exeunt.*

[Scene II. *Leonato's house.*]

*Enter Leonato and an old man [Antonio], brother
to Leonato.*

Leonato. How now, brother? Where is my cousin°
your son? Hath he provided this music?

Antonio. He is very busy about it. But, brother, I can
tell you strange news that you yet dreamt not of.

5 *Leonato.* Are they° good?

Antonio. As the events stamps° them. But they have
a good cover, they show well outward. The Prince
and Count Claudio, walking in a thick-pleached
alley in mine orchard,° were thus much overheard
10 by a man of mine. The Prince discovered° to Claudio that he loved my niece your daughter and meant
to acknowledge it this night in a dance, and if he
found her accordant,° he meant to take the present
time by the top° and instantly break with you of it.

15 *Leonato.* Hath the fellow any wit that told you this?

I.ii.1 *cousin* kinsman   5 *they* i.e., the news (plural in the sixteenth
century)   6 *As the events stamps them* as the outcome proves them
to be (a plural noun, especially when felt to be singular, often has
a verb ending in -*s*)   8–9 *thick-pleached alley in mine orchard* walk
or arbor fenced by interwoven branches in my garden   10 *discovered* disclosed   13 *accordant* agreeing   14 *top* forelock

Antonio. A good sharp fellow. I will send for him, and
question him yourself.

Leonato. No, no. We will hold it as a dream till it
appear itself. But I will acquaint my daughter
withal, that she may be the better prepared for an   *20*
answer, if peradventure this be true. Go you and
tell her of it.

[*Enter Attendants.*]

Cousin, you know what you have to do. O, I cry
you mercy,° friend. Go you with me, and I will use
your skill. Good cousin, have a care this busy time.   *25*
Exeunt.

[Scene III. *Leonato's house.*]

*Enter Sir John the Bastard and Conrade, his
companion.*

Conrade. What the goodyear,° my lord! Why are you
thus out of measure sad?°

Don John. There is no measure in the occasion that
breeds; therefore the sadness is without limit.

Conrade. You should hear reason.   *5*

Don John. And when I have heard it, what blessing
brings it?

Conrade. If not a present remedy, at least a patient
sufferance.

Don John. I wonder that thou, being (as thou say'st   *10*
thou art) born under Saturn,° goest about to apply

23–24 *cry you mercy* beg your pardon   I.iii.1 *What the goodyear*
(an explive)   2 *out of measure sad* unduly morose   11 *under
Saturn* i.e., naturally sullen

a moral medicine to a mortifying mischief.° I cannot hide what I am. I must be sad when I have
cause, and smile at no man's jests; eat when I have
15 stomach, and wait for no man's leisure; sleep when
I am drowsy, and tend on no man's business; laugh
when I am merry, and claw no man in his humor.°

Conrade. Yea, but you must not make the full show
of this till you may do it without controlment. You
20 have of late stood out against your brother, and he
hath ta'en you newly into his grace, where it is impossible you should take true root but by the fair
weather that you make yourself. It is needful that
you frame° the season for your own harvest.

25 *Don John.* I had rather be a canker° in a hedge than
a rose in his grace, and it better fits my blood to be
disdained of all than to fashion a carriage° to rob
love from any. In this, though I cannot be said to
be a flattering honest man, it must not be denied
30 but I am a plain-dealing villain. I am trusted with
a muzzle and enfranchised with a clog; therefore I
have decreed not to sing in my cage. If I had my
mouth, I would bite; if I had my liberty, I would
do my liking. In the meantime let me be that I am,
35 and seek not to alter me.

Conrade. Can you make no use of your discontent?

Don John. I make all use of it, for I use it only. Who
comes here?

Enter Borachio.

What news, Borachio?

40 *Borachio.* I came yonder from a great supper. The
Prince your brother is royally entertained by Leonato, and I can give you intelligence° of an intended
marriage.

12 *mortifying mischief* killing calamity   17 *claw no man in his
humor* i.e., flatter no man (*claw* = pat or scratch on the back; *humor*
= whim)   24 *frame* bring about   25 *canker* wild rose   27 *fashion
a carriage* contrive a behavior   42 *intelligence* information

Don John. Will it serve for any model to build mischief on? What is he for a fool that betroths himself to unquietness?   *45*

Borachio. Marry,° it is your brother's right hand.

Don John. Who? The most exquisite Claudio?

Borachio. Even he.

Don John. A proper squire!° And who? And who?   *50*
Which way looks he?

Borachio. Marry, one Hero, the daughter and heir of
Leonato.

Don John. A very forward March-chick!° How came
you to this?   *55*

Borachio. Being entertained for° a perfumer, as I was
smoking° a musty room, comes me the Prince and
Claudio, hand in hand in sad° conference. I whipped
me behind the arras and there heard it agreed upon
that the Prince should woo Hero for himself, and   *60*
having obtained her, give her to Count Claudio.

Don John. Come, come, let us thither. This may prove
food to my displeasure. That young start-up hath
all the glory of my overthrow. If I can cross him
any way, I bless myself every way. You are both   *65*
sure,° and will assist me?

Conrade. To the death, my lord.

Don John. Let us to the great supper. Their cheer is
the greater that I am subdued. Would the cook
were o' my mind! Shall we go prove° what's to be   *70*
done?

Borachio. We'll wait upon your lordship.
                                        Exit [with others].

47 *Marry* (an expletive, from "by the Virgin Mary")   50 *proper
squire* fine young fellow   54 *forward March-chick* precocious fellow
(i.e., born in early spring)   56 *entertained for* employed as   57
smoking fumigating (or possibly merely perfuming)   58 *sad* serious
66 *sure* reliable   70 *prove* try

[ACT II

Scene I. *Leonato's house.*]

Enter Leonato, his brother [Antonio], Hero his daughter, and Beatrice his niece, [also Margaret and Ursula].

Leonato. Was not Count John here at supper?

Antonio. I saw him not.

Beatrice. How tartly that gentleman looks! I never can see him but I am heartburned an hour after.

5 *Hero.* He is of a very melancholy° disposition.

Beatrice. He were an excellent man that were made just in the midway between him and Benedick. The one is too like an image and says nothing, and the other too like my lady's eldest son,° evermore
10 tattling.

Leonato. Then half Signior Benedick's tongue in Count John's mouth, and half Count John's melancholy in Signior Benedick's face—

Beatrice. With a good leg and a good foot,° uncle, and
15 money enough in his purse, such a man would win any woman in the world, if'a could get her good will.

II.i.5 *melancholy* ill-tempered   9 *eldest son* i.e., overly confident (as heir presumptive)   14 *foot* (perhaps with a pun on French *foutre*, to copulate—i.e., a good lover)

Leonato. By my troth, niece, thou wilt never get thee
a husband if thou be so shrewd° of thy tongue.

Antonio. In faith, she's too curst.°   20

Beatrice. Too curst is more than curst. I shall lessen
God's sending that way, for it is said, "God sends
a curst cow short horns"; but to a cow too curst he
sends none.

Leonato. So, by being too curst, God will send you no   25
horns.°

Beatrice. Just,° if he send me no husband; for the
which blessing I am at him upon my knees every
morning and evening. Lord, I could not endure a
husband with a beard on his face. I had rather lie   30
in the woolen!°

Leonato. You may light on a husband that hath no
beard.

Beatrice. What should I do with him? Dress him in
my apparel and make him my waiting gentle-   35
woman? He that hath a beard is more than a youth,
and he that hath no beard is less than a man; and
he that is more than a youth is not for me; and he
that is less than a man, I am not for him. Therefore
I will even take sixpence in earnest° of the berrord°   40
and lead his apes into hell.°

Leonato. Well then, go you into hell?

Beatrice. No; but to the gate, and there will the devil
meet me like an old cuckold with horns on his head,
and say, "Get you to heaven, Beatrice, get you to   45
heaven. Here's no place for you maids." So deliver
I up my apes, and away to Saint Peter. For the

19 *shrewd* sharp   20 *curst* shrewish   25–26 *no horns* (i.e., horn
used as phallic symbol, as Beatrice's next remark makes plain)   27
just exactly   31 *in the woolen* between scratchy blankets   40 *in
earnest* (1) advance payment (2) in all seriousness   40 *berrord*
bearward, animal keeper   41 *lead his apes into hell* traditional punishment for dying unwed

heavens, he shows me where the bachelors° sit, and there live we as merry as the day is long.

50 *Antonio.* [*To Hero*] Well, niece, I trust you will be ruled by your father.

Beatrice. Yes, faith. It is my cousin's duty to make cursy° and say, "Father, as it please you." But yet for all that, cousin, let him be a handsome fellow,

55 or else make another cursy, and say, "Father, as it please me."

Leonato. [*To Beatrice*] Well, niece, I hope to see you one day fitted° with a husband.

Beatrice. Not till God make men of some other metal°

60 than earth. Would it not grieve a woman to be overmastered with a piece of valiant dust? To make an account of her life to a clod of wayward marl?° No, uncle, I'll none. Adam's sons are my brethren, and truly I hold it a sin to match in my kindred.

65 *Leonato.* Daughter, remember what I told you. If the Prince do solicit you in that kind, you know your answer.

Beatrice. The fault will be in the music, cousin, if you be not wooed in good time. If the Prince be too

70 important,° tell him there is measure° in every-thing, and so dance out the answer. For, hear me, Hero: wooing, wedding, and repenting is as a Scotch jig, a measure, and a cinquepace.° The first suit is hot and hasty like a Scotch jig (and full as

75 fantastical); the wedding, mannerly modest, as a measure, full of state and ancientry; and then comes Repentance and with his bad legs falls into the

---

48 *bachelors* unwed persons (female as well as male) 53 *cursy* curtsy
58 *fitted* (continues playful sexual innuendo of the scene) 59 *metal*
substance   62 *marl* earth 70 *important* importunate 70 *measure*
(1) discernible time sequence (2) moderation (the entire speech is a
light parody of Sir John Davies' *Orchestra, A Poem of Dancing*
[1596]; cf. stanza 23: "Time the measure of all moving is/And
dancing is a moving all in measure") 73 *cinquepace* lively dance

cinquepace faster and faster, till he sink into his
grave.

Leonato. Cousin, you apprehend passing shrewdly.   80

Beatrice. I have a good eye, uncle; I can see a church
by daylight.

Leonato. The revelers are ent'ring, brother. Make
good room.

[*All put on their masks.*]

*'Enter Prince [Don] Pedro, Claudio, and Bene-
dick, and Balthasar [masked; and without masks
Borachio and] Don John.*

Don Pedro. Lady, will you walk about with your   85
friend?°

Hero. So you walk softly and look sweetly and say
nothing, I am yours for the walk; and especially
when I walk away.

Don Pedro. With me in your company?   90

Hero. I may say so when I please.

Don Pedro. And when please you to say so?

Hero. When I like your favor,° for God defend° the
lute should be like the case!°

Don Pedro. My visor° is Philemon's° roof; within the   95
house is Jove.

Hero. Why then, your visor should be thatched.

Don Pedro. Speak low if you speak love.

[*Draws her aside.*]

Benedick.° Well, I would you did like me.

86 *friend* lover   93 *favor* face   93 *defend* forbid   93–94 *the lute
. . . case* i.e., your face be as ugly as your mask   95 *visor* mask
95 *Philemon* peasant who entertained Jove in his house   99 *Benedick* (many editors emend the Quarto, and give this and Benedick's
two subsequent speeches to Balthasar; but in V.ii Benedick and
Margaret spar, and they may well do so here)

100 *Margaret*. So would not I for your own sake, for I
have many ill qualities.

Benedick. Which is one?

Margaret. I say my prayers aloud.

Benedick. I love you the better. The hearers may cry
105 amen.

Margaret. God match me with a good dancer!

Balthasar. [*Interposing*] Amen.

Margaret. And God keep him out of my sight when
the dance is done! Answer, clerk.

110 *Balthasar*. No more words. The clerk is answered.

Ursula. I know you well enough. You are Signior
Antonio.

Antonio. At a word, I am not.

Ursula. I know you by the waggling° of your head.

115 *Antonio*. To tell you true, I counterfeit him.

Ursula. You could never do him so ill-well unless you
were the very man. Here's his dry° hand up and
down. You are he, you are he!

Antonio. At a word I am not.

120 *Ursula*. Come, come, do you think I do not know you
by your excellent wit? Can virtue hide itself? Go to,
mum, you are he. Graces will appear, and there's
an end.

Beatrice. Will you not tell me who told you so?

125 *Benedick*. No, you shall pardon me.

Beatrice. Nor will you not tell me who you are?

Benedick. Not now.

Beatrice. That I was disdainful, and that I had my

114 *waggling* i.e., palsy   117 *dry* dried-up (with age)

good wit out of the "Hundred Merry Tales."° Well,
this was Signior Benedick that said so. 130

Benedick. What's he?

Beatrice. I am sure you know him well enough.

Benedick. Not I, believe me.

Beatrice. Did he never make you laugh?

Benedick. I pray you, what is he? 135

Beatrice. Why, he is the Prince's jester, a very dull
fool. Only his° gift is in devising impossible slanders. None but libertines delight in him, and the
commendation is not in his wit, but in his villainy;
for he both pleases men and angers them, and then 140
they laugh at him and beat him. I am sure he is in
the fleet;° I would he had boarded me.

Benedick. When I know the gentleman, I'll tell him
what you say.

Beatrice. Do, do. He'll but break a comparison or two 145
on me; which peradventure (not marked or not
laughed at), strikes him into melancholy, and then
there's a partridge wing saved, for the fool will eat
no supper that night. [*Music.*] We must follow the
leaders. 150

Benedick. In every good thing.

Beatrice. Nay, if they lead to any ill, I will leave them
at the next turning.

> *Dance. Exeunt [all except Don John,*
> *Borachio and Claudio].*

Don John. Sure my brother is amorous on Hero and
hath withdrawn her father to break with him about 155
it. The ladies follow her and but one visor remains.

---

129 *Hundred Merry Tales* a popular collection of amusing, coarse
anecdotes 137 *Only his* his only 142 *fleet* group (the related
meaning, group of ships, leads to *boarded me,* but perhaps too there
is an allusion to Fleet Prison)

Borachio. And that is Claudio. I know him by his bearing.

Don John. Are not you Signior Benedick?

160 *Claudio.* You know me well. I am he.

Don John. Signior, you are very near my brother in his love. He is enamored on Hero. I pray you dissuade him from her; she is no equal for his birth. You may do the part of an honest man in it.

165 *Claudio.* How know you he loves her?

Don John. I heard him swear his affection.

Borachio. So did I too, and he swore he would marry her tonight.

Don John. Come, let us to the banquet.°

Exeunt. Manet Claudio.

170 *Claudio.* Thus answer I in name of Benedick
But hear these ill news with the ears of Claudio.
'Tis certain so. The Prince woos for himself.
Friendship is constant in all other things
Save in the office° and affairs of love.
175 Therefore all hearts in love use their own tongues;
Let every eye negotiate for itself
And trust no agent; for beauty is a witch
Against whose charms faith melteth into blood.°
This is an accident of hourly proof,°
180 Which I mistrusted not. Farewell therefore Hero!

Enter Benedick.

Benedick. Count Claudio?

Claudio. Yea, the same.

Benedick. Come, will you go with me?

---

169 *banquet* light meal, or course, of fruit, wine, and dessert   174 *office* business   178 *blood* passion, desire   179 *accident of hourly proof* common happening

Claudio. Whither?

Benedick. Even to the next° willow,° about your own   185
business, County.° What fashion will you wear the
garland of? About your neck, like an usurer's chain?
Or under your arm, like a lieutenant's scarf? You
must wear it one way, for the Prince hath got your
Hero.   190

Claudio. I wish him joy of her.

Benedick. Why, that's spoken like an honest drovier.°
So they sell bullocks. But did you think the Prince
would have served you thus?

Claudio. I pray you leave me.   195

Benedick. Ho! Now you strike like the blind man!
'Twas the boy that stole your meat, and you'll beat
the post.°

Claudio. If it will not be, I'll leave you.   *Exit.*

Benedick. Alas, poor hurt fowl! Now will he creep   200
into sedges. But, that my Lady Beatrice should
know me, and not know me! The Prince's fool! Ha!
It may be I go under that title because I am merry.
Yea, but so I am apt to do myself wrong. I am not
so reputed. It is the base (though bitter) disposi-   205
tion of Beatrice that puts the world into her person
and so gives me out.° Well, I'll be revenged as I
may.

Enter the Prince [Don Pedro], Hero, Leonato.

Don Pedro. Now, signior, where's the Count? Did you   210
see him?

Benedick. Troth, my lord, I have played the part of
Lady Fame.° I found him here as melancholy as a

185 *next* nearest 185 *willow* symbol of unrequited love 186
County Count 192 *drovier* cattle dealer 197–98 *beat the post* i.e.,
strike out blindly 205–07 *It is . . . gives me out* it is the low and
harsh disposition of Beatrice to assume her opinion of me is the
world's opinion of me 212 *Lady Fame* goddess of rumor

lodge in a warren.° I told him, and I think I told
him true, that your Grace had got the good will of
215 this young lady, and I off'red him my company to
a willow tree, either to make him a garland, as being
forsaken, or to bind him up a rod, as being worthy
to be whipped.

Don Pedro. To be whipped? What's his fault?

220 *Benedick.* The flat transgression of a schoolboy who,
being overjoyed with finding a bird's nest, shows it
his companion, and he steals it.

Don Pedro. Wilt thou make a trust a transgression?
The transgression is in the stealer.

225 *Benedick.* Yet it had not been amiss the rod had been
made, and the garland too; for the garland he might
have worn himself, and the rod he might have bestowed on you, who (as I take it) have stol'n his
bird's nest.

230 *Don Pedro.* I will but teach them to sing and restore
them to the owner.

Benedick. If their singing answer your saying, by my
faith you say honestly.

Don Pedro. The Lady Beatrice hath a quarrel to you.
235 The gentleman that danced with her told her she
is much wronged by you.

Benedick. O, she misused me past the endurance of a
block! An oak but with one green leaf on it would
have answered her; my very visor began to assume
240 life and scold with her. She told me, not thinking I
had been myself, that I was the Prince's jester, that
I was duller than a great thaw; huddling jest upon
jest with such impossible conveyance° upon me
that I stood like a man at a mark,° with a whole
245 army shooting at me. She speaks poniards, and
every word stabs. If her breath were as terrible as

213 *in a warren* i.e., in a lonely place   243 *impossible conveyance*
incredible dexterity   244 *mark* target

her terminations,° there were no living near her;
she would infect to the North Star. I would not
marry her though she were endowed with all that
Adam had left him before he transgressed. She   250
would have made Hercules have turned spit, yea,
and have cleft his club to make the fire too. Come,
talk not of her. You shall find her the infernal Ate°
in good apparel. I would to God some scholar
would conjure her,° for certainly, while she is here,   255
a man may live as quiet in hell as in a sanctuary;
and people sin upon purpose, because they would
go thither; so indeed all disquiet, horror, and per-
turbation follows her.

Enter Claudio and Beatrice.

Don Pedro. Look, here she comes.   260

Benedick. Will your Grace command me any service
to the world's end? I will go on the slightest errand
now to the Antipodes that you can devise to send
me on; I will fetch you a toothpicker now from the
furthest inch of Asia; bring you the length of Prester   265
John's° foot; fetch you a hair off the great Cham's°
beard; do you any embassage to the Pygmies—
rather than hold three words' conference with this
harpy. You have no employment for me?

Don Pedro. None, but to desire your good company.   270

Benedick. O God, sir, here's a dish I love not! I cannot
endure my Lady Tongue.   *Exit.*

Don Pedro. Come, lady, come; you have lost the heart
of Signior Benedick.

Beatrice. Indeed, my lord, he lent it me awhile, and I   275
gave him use° for it, a double heart for his single
one. Marry, once before he won it of me with false

247 *terminations* words   253 *Ate* goddess of discord   255 *conjure
her* i.e., exorcise the devil out of her   26 66 *Prester John* legendary
Christian king in remote Asia   266 *Cham* Khan   276 *use* interest

dice; therefore your Grace may well say I have
lost it.

280 *Don Pedro.* You have put him down, lady; you have
put him down.

Beatrice. So I would not he should do me, my lord,
lest I should prove the mother of fools.° I have
brought Count Claudio, whom you sent me to seek.

285 *Don Pedro.* Why, how now, Count? Wherefore are
you sad?

Claudio. Not sad, my lord.

Don Pedro. How then? Sick?

Claudio. Neither, my lord.

290 *Beatrice.* The Count is neither sad, nor sick, nor
merry, nor well; but civil Count, civil° as an orange,
and something of that jealous complexion.°

Don Pedro. I' faith, lady, I think your blazon° to be
true; though I'll be sworn, if he be so, his conceit°
295 is false. Here, Claudio, I have wooed in thy name,
and fair Hero is won. I have broke with her father,
and his good will obtained. Name the day of marriage, and God give thee joy!

Leonato. Count, take of me my daughter, and with
300 her my fortunes. His Grace hath made the match,
and all grace say amen to it!

Beatrice. Speak, Count, 'tis your cue.

Claudio. Silence is the perfectest herald of joy. I were
but little happy if I could say how much. Lady, as
305 you are mine, I am yours. I give away myself for
you and dote upon the exchange.

Beatrice. Speak, cousin; or (if you cannot) stop his
mouth with a kiss and let not him speak neither.

---

283 *fools* babies   291 *civil* polite (with a pun on orange of Seville)
292 *complexion* (1) disposition (2) color (i.e., yellowish for jealousy)
293 *blazon* description   294 *conceit* idea, concept

Don Pedro. In faith, lady, you have a merry heart.

Beatrice. Yea, my lord; I thank it, poor fool, it keeps   *310*
on the windy° side of care. My cousin tells him in
his ear that he is in her heart.

Claudio. And so she doth, cousin.

Beatrice. Good Lord, for alliance! Thus goes everyone to the world but I, and I am sunburnt.° I may   *315*
sit in a corner and cry "Heigh-ho for a husband!"

Don Pedro. Lady Beatrice, I will get you one.

Beatrice. I would rather have one of your father's
getting.° Hath your Grace ne'er a brother like you?
Your father got excellent husbands, if a maid could   *320*
come by them.

Don Pedro. Will you have me, lady?

Beatrice. No, my lord, unless I might have another for
working days; your Grace is too costly to wear
every day. But I beseech your Grace pardon me.   *325*
I was born to speak all mirth and no matter.

Don Pedro. Your silence most offends me, and to be
merry best becomes you, for out o' question you
were born in a merry hour.

Beatrice. No, sure, my lord, my mother cried; but   *330*
then there was a star danced, and under that was
I born. Cousins, God give you joy!

Leonato. Niece, will you look to those things I told
you of?

Beatrice. I cry you mercy,° uncle. By your Grace's   *335*
pardon.

                             Exit Beatrice.

Don Pedro. By my troth, a pleasant-spirited lady.

---

311 *windy* windward, safe   314–15 *Good Lord . . . sunburnt* i.e.,
everyone gets a husband but me, and I am ugly (*sunburnt* = tanned,
and therefore ugly in the sixteenth century)   319 *getting* begetting
335 *cry you mercy* beg your pardon

Leonato. There's little of the melancholy element in
   her, my lord. She is never sad but when she sleeps,
340 and not ever° sad then; for I have heard my daughter say she hath often dreamt of unhappiness and
   waked herself with laughing.

Don Pedro. She cannot endure to hear tell of a husband.

345 *Leonato.* O, by no means! She mocks all her wooers
   out of suit.

Don Pedro. She were an excellent wife for Benedick.

Leonato. O Lord, my lord! If they were but a week
   married, they would talk themselves mad.

350 *Don Pedro.* County Claudio, when mean you to go to
   church?

Claudio. Tomorrow, my lord. Time goes on crutches
   till Love have all his rites.

Leonato. Not till Monday, my dear son, which is hence
355 a just sevennight; and a time too brief too, to have
   all things answer my mind.

Don Pedro. Come, you shake the head at so long a
   breathing; but I warrant thee, Claudio, the time
   shall not go dully by us. I will in the interim un-
360 dertake one of Hercules' labors, which is, to bring
   Signior Benedick and the Lady Beatrice into a
   mountain of affection th' one with th' other. I would
   fain have it a match, and I doubt not but to fashion
   it if you three will but minister such assistance as
365 I shall give you direction.

Leonato. My lord, I am for you, though it cost me ten
   nights' watchings.°

Claudio. And I, my lord.

Don Pedro. And you too, gentle Hero?

340 *ever* always   366–67 *ten nights' watchings* ten nights awake

Hero. I will do any modest office, my lord, to help my 370
cousin to a good husband.

Don Pedro. And Benedick is not the unhopefullest
husband that I know. Thus far can I praise him: he
is of a noble strain, of approved° valor and confirmed honesty. I will teach you how to humor your 375
cousin, that she shall fall in love with Benedick;
and I [*to Leonato and Claudio*], with your two
helps, will so practice on° Benedick that, in despite
of his quick wit and his queasy stomach, he shall
fall in love with Beatrice. If we can do this, Cupid 380
is no longer an archer; his glory shall be ours, for
we are the only love-gods. Go in with me, and I
will tell you my drift.

Exit [*with the others*].

[Scene II. *Leonato's house.*]

Enter [*Don*] *John and Borachio.*

Don John. It is so. The Count Claudio shall marry the
daughter of Leonato.

Borachio. Yea, my lord; but I can cross it.

Don John. Any bar, any cross, any impediment will
be medicinable to me. I am sick in displeasure to 5
him, and whatsoever comes athwart his affection
ranges evenly° with mine. How canst thou cross
this marriage?

Borachio. Not honestly, my lord; but so covertly that
no dishonesty shall appear in me. 10

Don John. Show me briefly how.

374 *approved* tested   378 *practice on* deceive   II.ii.7 *ranges evenly*
goes in a straight line (i.e., suits me exactly)

Borachio. I think I told your lordship, a year since,
how much I am in the favor of Margaret, the waiting gentlewoman to Hero.

15 *Don John.* I remember.

Borachio. I can, at any unseasonable instant of the
night, appoint her to look out at her lady's chamber
window.

Don John. What life is in that to be the death of this
20   marriage?

Borachio. The poison of that lies in you to temper. Go
you to the Prince your brother; spare not to tell
him that he hath wronged his honor in marrying
the renowned Claudio (whose estimation do you
25   mightily hold up) to a contaminated stale,° such
a one as Hero.

Don John. What proof shall I make of that?

Borachio. Proof enough to misuse the Prince, to vex
Claudio, to undo Hero, and kill Leonato. Look you
30   for any other issue?

Don John. Only to despite them I will endeavor anything.

Borachio. Go then; find me a meet hour° to draw Don
Pedro and the Count Claudio alone; tell them that
35   you know that Hero loves me; intend° a kind of
zeal both to the Prince and Claudio (as in love of
your brother's honor, who hath made this match,
and his friend's reputation, who is thus like to be
cozened° with the semblance of a maid) that you
40   have discovered thus. They will scarcely believe
this without trial. Offer them instances;° which
shall bear no less likelihood than to see me at her
chamber window, hear me call Margaret Hero, hear
Margaret term me Claudio; and bring them to see
45   this the very night before the intended wedding.

25 *stale* prostitute   33 *meet hour* suitable time   35 *intend* pretend
39 *cozened* cheated   41 *instances* proofs

For in the meantime I will so fashion the matter
that Hero shall be absent; and there shall appear
such seeming truth of Hero's disloyalty that jeal-   50
ousy° shall be called assurance and all the preparation overthrown.

Don John. Grow this to what adverse issue it can, I
will put it in practice. Be cunning in the working
this, and thy fee is a thousand ducats.

Borachio. Be you constant in the accusation, and my
cunning shall not shame me.   55

Don John. I will presently go learn their day of marriage.

                              Exit [with Borachio].

[Scene III. *Leonato's garden.*]

Enter Benedick alone.

Benedick. Boy!

[*Enter Boy.*]

Boy. Signior?

Benedick. In my chamber window lies a book. Bring it
hither to me in the orchard.°

Boy. I am here already, sir.   5

Benedick. I know that, but I would have thee hence
and here again. (*Exit [Boy].*) I do much wonder
that one man, seeing how much another man is a
fool when he dedicates his behaviors to love, will,
after he hath laughed at such shallow follies in   10
others, become the argument° of his own scorn by

48–49 *jealousy* mistrust   II.iii.3 *orchard* garden   11 *argument* subject matter

falling in love; and such a man is Claudio. I have
known when there was no music with him but the
drum and the fife; and now had he rather hear the
tabor and the pipe.° I have known when he would
have walked ten mile afoot to see a good armor; and
now will he lie ten nights awake carving the fashion°
of a new doublet. He was wont to speak plain and
to the purpose, like an honest man and a soldier;
and now is he turned orthography;° his words are
a very fantastical banquet—just so many strange
dishes. May I be so converted and see with these
eyes? I cannot tell; I think not. I will not be sworn
but love may transform me to an oyster; but I'll take
my oath on it, till he have made an oyster of me he
shall never make me such a fool. One woman is fair,
yet I am well; another is wise, yet I am well; another
virtuous, yet I am well. But till all graces be in one
woman, one woman shall not come in my grace.
Rich she shall be, that's certain; wise, or I'll none;
virtuous, or I'll never cheapen° her; fair, or I'll never
look on her; mild, or come not near me; noble, or
not I for an angel;° of good discourse,° an excellent
musician, and her hair shall be of what color it
please God. Ha, the Prince and Monsieur Love!
[*Retiring*] I will hide me in the arbor.

*Enter Prince [Don Pedro], Leonato, Claudio,
[to the sound of] music.*

Don Pedro. Come, shall we hear this music?

Claudio. Yea, my good lord. How still the evening is,
As hushed on purpose to grace harmony!

Don Pedro. See you where Benedick hath hid himself?

---

15 *tabor and the pipe* music of an unmartial sort   17 *carving the
fashion* considering the design   20 *orthography* i.e., into a pedant (?)
31 *cheapen* bargain for   32–33 *noble . . . angel* (puns: both words
are Elizabethan coins)   33 *discourse* conversation

Claudio. O, very well, my lord. The music ended,
  We'll fit the kid fox with a pennyworth.°

Enter Balthasar with music.

Don Pedro. Come, Balthasar, we'll hear that song
  again.

Balthasar. O, good my lord, tax not so bad a voice
  To slander music any more than once.   *45*

Don Pedro. It is the witness still of excellency
  To put a strange face on his own perfection.
  I pray thee sing, and let me woo no more.

Balthasar. Because you talk of wooing, I will sing,
  Since many a wooer doth commence his suit   *50*
  To her he thinks not worthy, yet he woos,
  Yet will he swear he loves.

Don Pedro.   Nay, pray thee come;
  Or if thou wilt hold longer argument,
  Do it in notes.

Balthasar.   Note this before my notes:
  There's not a note of mine that's worth the noting.   *55*

Don Pedro. Why, these are very crotchets° that he
  speaks!
  Note notes, forsooth, and nothing!°   [*Music.*]

Benedick. [*Aside*] Now divine air! Now is his soul
  ravished! Is it not strange that sheep's guts should
  hale souls out of men's bodies? Well, a horn for my   *60*
  money, when all's done.   [*Balthasar sings.*]

The Song

Sigh no more, ladies, sigh no more,
  Men were deceivers ever,

---

42 *We'll . . . pennyworth* i.e., we'll give Benedick a little something
(perhaps *kid fox* means "young fox," perhaps "known fox")   56
crotchets (1) whims (2) musical notes   57 *nothing* (pronounced
"noting," hence a pun)

> One foot in sea, and one on shore,
> 65   To one thing constant never.
>   Then sigh not so,
>   But let them go,
>   And be you blithe and bonny,
> Converting all your sounds of woe
> 70   Into hey nonny, nonny.
>
> Sing no more ditties, sing no moe,
>   Of dumps° so dull and heavy;
> The fraud of men was ever so,
>   Since summer first was leavy.
> 75   Then sigh not so, &c.

Don Pedro. By my troth, a good song.

Balthasar. And an ill singer, my lord.

Don Pedro. Ha, no, no, faith! Thou sing'st well enough
for a shift.°

80 *Benedick.* [*Aside*] And he had been a dog that should
have howled thus, they would have hanged him; and
I pray God his bad voice bode no mischief. I had as
live° have heard the night raven, come what plague
could have come after it.

85 *Don Pedro.* Yea, marry. Dost thou hear, Balthasar? I
pray thee get us some excellent music; for tomorrow
night we would have it at the Lady Hero's chamber
window.

Balthasar. The best I can, my lord.

90 *Don Pedro.* Do so. Farewell.
                    Exit Balthasar [*with Musicians*].

Come hither, Leonato. What was it you told me of
today? That your niece Beatrice was in love with
Signior Benedick?

Claudio. O, ay! [*In a low voice to Don Pedro*] Stalk on,

---

72 *dumps* sad songs   79 *shift* makeshift   83 *live* lief

stalk on; the fowl sits. [*In full voice*] I did never 95
think that lady would have loved any man.

Leonato. No, nor I neither; but most wonderful that
she should so dote on Signior Benedick, whom she
hath in all outward behaviors seemed ever to abhor.

Benedick. [*Aside*] Is't possible? Sits the wind in that 100
corner?

Leonato. By my troth, my lord, I cannot tell what to
think of it, but that she loves him with an enraged
affection, it is past the infinite of thought.

Don Pedro. May be she doth but counterfeit. 105

Claudio. Faith, like enough.

Leonato. O God, counterfeit? There was never counterfeit of passion came so near the life of passion as
she discovers° it.

Don Pedro. Why, what effects of passion shows she? 110

Claudio. [*In a low voice*] Bait the hook well! This fish
will bite.

Leonato. What effects, my lord? She will sit you, you
heard my daughter tell you how.

Claudio. She did indeed. 115

Don Pedro. How, how, I pray you? You amaze me!
I would have thought her spirit had been invincible
against all assaults of affection.

Leonato. I would have sworn it had, my lord—especially against Benedick. 120

Benedick. [*Aside*] I should think this a gull° but that
the white-bearded fellow speaks it. Knavery cannot,
sure, hide himself in such reverence.

Claudio. [*In a low voice*] He hath ta'en th' infection;
hold° it up. 125

109 *discovers* reveals, betrays   121 *gull* trick   125 *hold* keep

Don Pedro. Hath she made her affection known to Benedick?

Leonato. No, and swears she never will. That's her torment.

130 *Claudio.* 'Tis true indeed. So your daughter says. "Shall I," says she, "that have so oft encount'red him with scorn, write to him that I love him?"

Leonato. This says she now when she is beginning to write to him; for she'll be up twenty times a night,
135 and there will she sit in her smock till she have writ a sheet of paper. My daughter tells us all.

Claudio. Now you talk of a sheet of paper, I remember a pretty jest your daughter told us of.

Leonato. O, when she had writ it, and was reading it
140 over, she found "Benedick" and "Beatrice" between the sheet?

Claudio. That.

Leonato. O, she tore the letter into a thousand half-pence,° railed at herself that she should be so im-
145 modest to write to one that she knew would flout her. "I measure him," says she, "by my own spirit; for I should flout him if he writ to me. Yea, though I love him, I should."

Claudio. Then down upon her knees she falls, weeps,
150 sobs, beats her heart, tears her hair, prays, curses— "O sweet Benedick! God give me patience!"

Leonato. She doth indeed; my daughter says so; and the ecstasy° hath so much overborne her that my daughter is sometime afeard she will do a des-
155 perate outrage to herself. It is very true.

Don Pedro. It were good that Benedick knew of it by some other, if she will not discover it.

143–44 *halfpence* i.e., small pieces   153 *ecstasy* madness

Claudio. To what end? He would make but a sport of
  it and torment the poor lady worse.

Don Pedro. And he should, it were an alms° to hang 160
  him! She's an excellent sweet lady, and, out of all
  suspicion, she is virtuous.

Claudio. And she is exceeding wise.

Don Pedro. In everything but in loving Benedick.

Leonato. O, my lord, wisdom and blood° combating 165
  in so tender a body, we have ten proofs to one that
  blood hath the victory. I am sorry for her, as I have
  just cause, being her uncle and her guardian.

Don Pedro. I would she had bestowed this dotage on
  me; I would have daffed all other respects° and 170
  made her half myself. I pray you tell Benedick of it
  and hear what'a will say.

Leonato. Were it good, think you?

Claudio. Hero thinks surely she will die; for she says
  she will die if he love her not, and she will die ere 175
  she make her love known, and she will die, if he
  woo her, rather than she will bate° one breath of
  her accustomed crossness.

Don Pedro. She doth well. If she should make tender°
  of her love, 'tis very possible he'll scorn it; for the 180
  man, as you know all, hath a contemptible° spirit.

Claudio. He is a very proper° man.

Don Pedro. He hath indeed a good outward happiness.

Claudio. Before God, and in my mind, very wise.

Don Pedro. He doth indeed show some sparks that are 185
  like wit.°

Claudio. And I take him to be valiant.

160 *an alms* a charity   165 *blood* passion   170 *daffed all other re-*
spects put aside all other considerations (i.e., of disparity in rank)
177 *bate* abate, give up   179 *tender* offer   181 *contemptible* disdainful   182 *proper* handsome   186 *wit* intelligence

Don Pedro. As Hector, I assure you. And in the man-
aging of quarrels you may say he is wise, for either
190   he avoids them with great discretion, or undertakes
them with a most Christianlike fear.

Leonato. If he do fear God, 'a must necessarily keep
peace. If he break the peace, he ought to enter into
a quarrel with fear and trembling.

195 *Don Pedro.* And so will he do; for the man doth fear
God, howsoever it seems not in him by some large
jests° he will make. Well, I am sorry for your niece.
Shall we go seek Benedick and tell him of her love?

Claudio. Never tell him, my lord; let her wear it out
200   with good counsel.

Leonato. Nay, that's impossible; she may wear her
heart out first.

Don Pedro. Well, we will hear further of it by your
daughter. Let it cool the while. I love Benedick well,
205   and I could wish he would modestly examine himself to see how much he is unworthy so good a lady.

Leonato. My lord, will you walk? Dinner is ready.
                                        [*They walk away.*]

Claudio. If he do not dote on her upon this, I will never
trust my expectation.

210 *Don Pedro.* Let there be the same net spread for her,
and that must your daughter and her gentlewomen
carry.° The sport will be, when they hold one an
opinion of another's dotage, and no such matter.
That's the scene that I would see, which will be
215   merely a dumb show.° Let us send her to call him
in to dinner.
                    [*Exeunt Don Pedro, Claudio, and Leonato.*]

Benedick. [*Advancing*] This can be no trick; the conference was sadly° borne. They have the truth of

196–97 *large jests* broad jokes   212 *carry* manage   215 *dumb show*
pantomime (because of embarrassment)   218 *sadly* seriously

this from Hero. They seem to pity the lady; it seems
her affections have their full bent.° Love me? Why, 220
it must be requited. I hear how I am censured. They
say I will bear myself proudly if I perceive the love
come from her. They say too that she will rather die
than give any sign of affection. I did never think to
marry; I must not seem proud. Happy are they that 225
hear their detractions and can put them to mending.
They say the lady is fair—'tis a truth, I can bear
them witness; and virtuous—'tis so, I cannot reprove
it; and wise, but for loving me; by my troth, it is
no addition to her wit, nor no great argument of her 230
folly; for I will be horribly in love with her. I may
chance have some odd quirks and remnants of wit
broken on me because I have railed so long against
marriage; but doth not the appetite alter? A man
loves the meat in his youth that he cannot endure 235
in his age. Shall quips and sentences° and these
paper bullets of the brain awe a man from the
career° of his humor? No, the world must be peo-
pled. When I said I would die a bachelor, I did not
think I should live till I were married. Here comes 240
Beatrice. By this day, she's a fair lady. I do spy
some marks of love in her.

Enter Beatrice.

Beatrice. Against my will I am sent to bid you come
in to dinner.

Benedick. Fair Beatrice, I thank you for your pains. 245

Beatrice. I took no more pains for those thanks than
you take pains to thank me. If it had been painful,
I would not have come.

Benedick. You take pleasure then in the message?

Beatrice. Yea, just so much as you may take upon a 250

---

220 *affections have their full bent* emotions are tightly stretched
(like a bent bow)　　236 *sentences* maxims　　238 *career* course

knife's point, and choke a daw withal.° You have
no stomach,° signior? Fare you well.   *Exit.*

Benedick. Ha! "Against my will I am sent to bid you
come in to dinner." There's a double meaning in
255 that. "I took no more pains for those thanks than
you took pains to thank me." That's as much as to
say, "Any pains that I take for you is as easy as
thanks." If I do not take pity of her, I am a villain;
if I do not love her, I am a Jew. I will go get her
260 picture.   *Exit.*

251 *withal* with   252 *no stomach* no wish to argue (as well as "no
appetite")

[ACT III

Scene I. *Leonato's garden.*]

*Enter Hero and two Gentlewomen, Margaret
and Ursula.*

Hero. Good Margaret, run thee to the parlor.
　There shalt thou find my cousin Beatrice
　Proposing with° the Prince and Claudio.
　Whisper her ear and tell her, I and Ursley
　Walk in the orchard, and our whole discourse　　　*5*
　Is all of her. Say that thou overheard'st us;
　And bid her steal into the pleachèd bower,
　Where honeysuckles, ripened by the sun,
　Forbid the sun to enter—like favorites,
　Made proud by princes, that advance their pride　　*10*
　Against that power that bred it.° There will she hide
　　her
　To listen our propose. This is thy office;°
　Bear thee well in it and leave us alone.

Margaret. I'll make her come, I warrant you, presently.
　　　　　　　　　　　　　　　　　　　　[*Exit.*]

Hero. Now, Ursula, when Beatrice doth come,　　　*15*
　As we do trace° this alley up and down,

III.i.3 *Proposing with* talking to　10–11 *Made proud . . . bred it*
(an Elizabethan audience of *c.*1600 would be reminded of the Earl
of Essex)　12 *office* duty　16 *trace* walk

Our talk must only be of Benedick.
When I do name him, let it be thy part
To praise him more than ever man did merit.
20 My talk to thee must be how Benedick
Is sick in love with Beatrice. Of this matter
Is little Cupid's crafty° arrow made,
That only° wounds by hearsay.

Enter Beatrice.

                                Now begin;
For look where Beatrice like a lapwing runs
25 Close by the ground, to hear our conference.

Ursula. The pleasant'st angling is to see the fish
Cut with her golden oars the silver stream
And greedily devour the treacherous bait;
So angle we for Beatrice, who even now
30 Is couchèd in the woodbine coverture.°
Fear you not my part of the dialogue.

Hero. Then go we near her, that her ear lose nothing
Of the false sweet bait that we lay for it.
                        [*They approach the bower.*]
No, truly, Ursula, she is too disdainful.
35 I know her spirits are as coy° and wild
As haggards° of the rock.

Ursula.   But are you sure
That Benedick loves Beatrice so entirely?

Hero. So says the Prince, and my new-trothèd lord.

Ursula. And did they bid you tell her of it, madam?

40 *Hero.* They did entreat me to acquaint her of it;
But I persuaded them, if they loved Benedick,
To wish him wrestle with affection
And never to let Beatrice know of it.

Ursula. Why did you so? Doth not the gentleman

22 *crafty* skillfully wrought   23 *only* solely   30 *woodbine cover-*
ture honeysuckle thicket   35 *coy* disdainful   36 *haggards* wild and
intractable hawks

    Deserve as full as fortunate a bed   45
    As ever Beatrice shall couch upon?

Hero. O god of love! I know he doth deserve
    As much as may be yielded to a man;
    But Nature never framed a woman's heart
    Of prouder stuff than that of Beatrice.   50
    Disdain and Scorn ride sparkling in her eyes,
    Misprizing° what they look on; and her wit
    Values itself so highly that to her
    All matter else seems weak. She cannot love,
    Nor take no shape nor project° of affection,   55
    She is so self-endeared.

Ursula.   Sure I think so;
    And therefore certainly it were not good
    She knew his love, lest she'll make sport at it.

Hero. Why, you speak truth. I never yet saw man,
    How wise, how noble, young, how rarely featured,   60
    But she would spell him backward. If fair-faced,
    She would swear the gentleman should be her sister;
    If black,° why, Nature, drawing of an antic,°
    Made a foul blot; if tall, a lance ill-headed;
    If low, an agate very vilely cut;°   65
    If speaking, why, a vane blown with all winds;
    If silent, why, a block movèd with none.
    So turns she every man the wrong side out
    And never gives to truth and virtue that
    Which simpleness and merit purchaseth.   70

Ursula. Sure, sure, such carping is not commendable.

Hero. No, not to be so odd, and from all fashions,°
    As Beatrice is, cannot be commendable.
    But who dare tell her so? If I should speak,
    She would mock me into air; O, she would laugh me   75
    Out of myself, press me to death with wit!
    Therefore let Benedick, like covered fire,

---

52 *Misprizing* despising   55 *project* notion   63 *black* dark-complexioned   63 *antic* grotesque figure   65 *agate very vilely cut* poorly done miniature   72 *from all fashions* contrary

Consume away in sighs, waste inwardly.
It were a better death than die with mocks,
80   Which is as bad as die with tickling.

Ursula. Yet tell her of it. Hear what she will say.

Hero. No; rather I will go to Benedick
And counsel him to fight against his passion.
And truly, I'll devise some honest° slanders
85   To stain my cousin with. One doth not know
How much an ill word may empoison liking.

Ursula. O, do not do your cousin such a wrong!
She cannot be so much without true judgment
(Having so swift and excellent a wit
90   As she is prized to have) as to refuse
So rare a gentleman as Signior Benedick.

Hero. He is the only man of Italy,
Always excepted my dear Claudio.

Ursula. I pray you be not angry with me, madam,
95   Speaking my fancy. Signior Benedick,
For shape, for bearing, argument, and valor,
Goes foremost in report through Italy.

Hero. Indeed he hath an excellent good name.

Ursula. His excellence did earn it ere he had it.
100   When are you married, madam?

Hero. Why, everyday tomorrow!° Come, go in.
I'll show thee some attires, and have thy counsel
Which is the best to furnish° me tomorrow.
                           [They walk away.]

Ursula. She's limed,° I warrant you! We have caught
her, madam.

105 *Hero.* If it prove so, then loving goes by haps;°
Some Cupid kills with arrows, some with traps.
                        [Exeunt Hero and Ursula.]

84 *honest* appropriate   101 *everyday tomorrow* i.e., tomorrow I
shall be married forever   103 *furnish* dress   104 *limed* caught (as
a bird is caught in birdlime, a sticky substance smeared on branches)
105 *haps* chance

Beatrice. [*Coming forward*] What fire is in mine ears?
      Can this be true?
      Stand I condemned for pride and scorn so much?
Contempt, farewell! And maiden pride, adieu!
      No glory lives behind the back of such.   *110*
And, Benedick, love on; I will requite thee,
      Taming my wild heart to thy loving hand.
If thou dost love, my kindness shall incite thee
      To bind our loves up in a holy band;
For others say thou dost deserve, and I   *115*
Believe it better than reportingly.°   *Exit.*

[Scene II. *Leonato's House.*]

Enter Prince [*Don Pedro*], *Claudio, Benedick,
      and Leonato.*

Don Pedro. I do but stay till your marriage be con-
summate, and then go I toward Aragon.

Claudio. I'll bring you thither, my lord, if you'll vouch-
safe° me.

Don Pedro. Nay, that would be as great a soil in the   *5*
new gloss of your marriage as to show a child his
new coat and forbid him to wear it. I will only be
bold with Benedick for his company; for, from the
crown of his head to the sole of his foot, he is all
mirth. He hath twice or thrice cut Cupid's bow-   *10*
string,° and the little hangman dare not shoot at him.
He hath a heart as sound as a bell; and his tongue
is the clapper, for what his heart thinks, his tongue
speaks.

Benedick. Gallants, I am not as I have been.   *15*

_____

116 *reportingly* i.e., mere hearsay   III.ii.3–4 *vouchsafe* permit   10–
11 *cut Cupid's bowstring* i.e., avoided falling in love   *i*

Leonato. So say I. Methinks you are sadder.°

Claudio. I hope he be in love.

Don Pedro. Hang him truant?° There's no true drop of
blood in him to be truly touched with love. If he be
20   sad, he wants money.

Benedick. I have the toothache.

Don Pedro. Draw it.°

Benedick. Hang it!

Claudio. You must hang it first and draw it afterwards.

25 *Don Pedro.* What? Sigh for the toothache?

Leonato. Where is but a humor or a worm.°

Benedick, Well, everyone cannot master a grief but
he that has it.°

Claudio. Yet say I he is in love.

30 *Don Pedro.* There is no appearance of fancy° in him,
unless it be a fancy that he hath to strange disguises;
as to be a Dutchman today, a Frenchman tomorrow; or in the shape of two countries at once, as a
German from the waist downward, all slops,° and
35   a Spaniard from the hip upward, no doublet.° Unless he have a fancy to this foolery, as it appears he
hath, he is no fool for fancy, as you would have
it appear he is.

Claudio. If he be not in love with some woman, there
40   is no believing old signs; 'a brushes his hat o'
mornings. What should that bode?

---

16 *sadder* graver   18 *truant* i.e., as unfaithful to his antiromantic
stance   22 *Draw it* extract it (but *draw* also means eviscerate;
traitors were hanged, drawn, and quartered. *Draw it* thus leads to
the exclamation *Hang it*)   26 *a humor or a worm* (supposed causes
of tooth decay, *humor* = secretion)   27–28 *Well . . . has it* i.e., a
man has to have a grief first before he can master it (Benedick does
not admit that he has a grief; but some editors emend *cannot* to
"can")   30 *fancy* love   34 *slops* loose breeches   35 *doublet* close-
fitting jacket

Don Pedro. Hath any man seen him at the barber's?

Claudio. No, but the barber's man hath been seen with him, and the old ornament of his cheek hath already stuffed tennis balls.° 45

Leonato. Indeed he looks younger than he did, by the loss of a beard.

Don Pedro. Nay, 'a rubs himself with civet.° Can you smell him out by that?

Claudio. That's as much as to say, the sweet youth's in love. 50

Don Pedro. The greatest note of it is his melancholy.

Claudio. And when was he wont to wash his face?

Don Pedro. Yea, or to paint himself?° For the which I hear what they say of him. 55

Claudio. Nay, but his jesting spirit, which is now crept into a lutestring, and now governed by stops.°

Don Pedro. Indeed that tells a heavy tale for him. Conclude, conclude, he is in love.

Claudio. Nay, but I know who loves him. 60

Don Pedro. That would I know too. I warrant, one that knows him not.

Claudio. Yes, and his ill conditions;° and in despite of all,° dies° for him.

Don Pedro. She shall be buried with her face upwards.° 65

Benedick. Yet is this no charm for the toothache. Old

44–45 *the old ornament . . . tennis balls* (cf. Beatrice's remark, II.i.29–30 "I could not endure a husband with a beard on his face") 48 *civet* perfume   54 *to paint himself* to use cosmetics   57 *stops* frets (on the lute)   63 *conditions* qualities   63–64 *in despite of all* notwithstanding   64 *dies* (1) pines away (2) is willing to "die" in the act of sex   65–66 *She shall . . . upwards* (continues sexual innuendo)

signior, walk aside with me; I have studied eight or
nine wise words to speak to you, which these hobby-
70 horses° must not hear.

                    [*Exeunt Benedick and Leonato.*]

Don Pedro. For my life, to break with him about Bea-
    trice!

Claudio. 'Tis even so. Hero and Margaret have by
    this played their parts with Beatrice, and then the
75   two bears will not bite one another when they meet.

Enter John the Bastard.

Don John. My lord and brother, God save you.

Don Pedro. Good den,° brother.

Don John. If your leisure served, I would speak with
    you.

80 *Don Pedro.* In private?

Don John. If it please you. Yet Count Claudio may
    hear, for what I would speak of concerns him.

Don Pedro. What's the matter?

Don John. [*To Claudio*] Means your lordship to be
85   married tomorrow?

Don Pedro. You know he does.

Don John. I know not that, when he knows what I
    know.

Claudio. If there be any impediment, I pray you dis-
90   cover it.

Don John. You may think I love you not; let that ap-
    pear hereafter, and aim better at me° by that° I
    now will manifest. For my brother (I think he holds
    you well, and in dearness of heart) hath holp to

69–70 *hobbyhorses* jokers (originally an imitation horse fastened
around the waist of a morris dancer)   77 *Good den* good evening
92 *aim better at me* judge better of me   92 *that* that which

effect your ensuing marriage—surely suit ill spent 95
and labor ill bestowed!

Don Pedro. Why, what's the matter?

Don John. I came hither to tell you, and, circum-
stances short'ned (for she has been too long a-talk-
ing of), the lady is disloyal.   100

Claudio. Who? Hero?

Don John. Even she—Leonato's Hero, your Hero,
every man's Hero.

Claudio. Disloyal?

Don John. The word is too good to paint out her wick- 105
edness. I could say she were worse. Think you of
a worse title, and I will fit her to it. Wonder not
till further warrant. Go but with me tonight, you
shall see her chamber window ent'red, even the
night before her wedding day. If you love her then, 110
tomorrow wed her. But it would better fit your
honor to change your mind.

Claudio. May this be so?

Don Pedro. I will not think it.

Don John. If you dare not trust that you see, confess 115
not that you know. If you will follow me, I will
show you enough; and when you have seen more
and heard more, proceed accordingly.

Claudio. If I see anything tonight why I should not
marry her tomorrow, in the congregation where I 120
should wed, there will I shame her.

Don Pedro. And, as I wooed for thee to obtain her, I
will join with thee to disgrace her.

Don John. I will disparage her no farther till you are
my witnesses. Bear it coldly° but till midnight, and 125
let the issue show itself.

125 *coldly* calmly

Don Pedro. O day untowardly turned!

Claudio. O mischief strangely thwarting!

Don John. O plague right well prevented! So will you
130   say when you have seen the sequel.   [*Exeunt.*]

[Scene III. A street.]

Enter Dogberry and his compartner [Verges,]
with the Watch.

Dogberry. Are you good men and true?

Verges. Yea, or else it were pity but they should suffer
salvation,° body and soul.

Dogberry. Nay, that were a punishment too good for
5   them if they should have any allegiance in them,
being chosen for the Prince's watch.

Verges. Well, give them their charge,° neighbor Dogberry.

Dogberry. First, who think you the most desartless
10   man to be constable?

First Watch. Hugh Oatcake, sir, or George Seacole,
for they can write and read.

Dogberry. Come hither, neighbor Seacole. God hath
blessed you with a good name. To be a well-favored°
15   man is the gift of fortune, but to write and read
comes by nature.

Second Watch. Both which, Master Constable—

Dogberry. You have; I knew it would be your answer.
Well, for your favor, sir, why, give God thanks and

III.iii.3 *salvation* damnation (the beginning of the malapropisms
basic to the comedy of Dogberry and Verges)   7 *charge* instructions
14 *well-favored* handsome

make no boast of it; and for your writing and read- 20
ing, let that appear when there is no need of such
vanity. You are thought here to be the most sense-
less and fit man for the constable of the watch.
Therefore bear you the lanthorn. This is your
charge: you shall comprehend all vagrom° men; 25
you are to bid any man stand,° in the Prince's
name.

Second Watch. How if 'a will not stand?

Dogberry. Why then, take no note of him, but let him
go, and presently call the rest of the watch together 30
and thank God you are rid of a knave.

Verges. If he will not stand when he is bidden, he is
none of the Prince's subjects.

Dogberry. True, and they are to meddle with none but
the Prince's subjects. You shall also make no noise 35
in the streets; for, for the watch to babble and to
talk is most tolerable, and not to be endured.

Watch.° We will rather sleep than talk; we know what
belongs to a watch.

Dogberry. Why, you speak like an ancient and most 40
quiet watchman, for I cannot see how sleeping
should offend. Only, have a care that your bills°
be not stol'n. Well, you are to call at all the ale-
houses and bid those that are drunk get them to
bed.   45

Watch. How if they will not?

Dogberry. Why then, let them alone till they are sober.
If they make you not then the better answer, you
may say they are not the men you took them for.

Watch. Well, sir.   50

---

25 *comprehend all vagrom* i.e., apprehend all vagrant   26 *stand*
halt, stop   38 *Watch* (neither the Quarto nor the Folio differenti-
ates again between First Watch and Second Watch until the end of
this scene)   42 *bills* constables' pikes

Dogberry. If you meet a thief, you may suspect him, by virtue of your office, to be no true man; and for such kind of men, the less you meddle or make with them, why, the more is for your honesty.

55 *Watch.* If we know him to be a thief, shall we not lay hands on him?

Dogberry. Truly, by your office you may; but I think they that touch pitch will be defiled. The most peaceable way for you, if you do take a thief, is to
60 let him show himself what he is, and steal out of your company.

Verges. You have been always called a merciful man, partner.

Dogberry. Truly, I would not hang a dog by my will,
65 much more a man who hath any honesty in him.

Verges. If you hear a child cry in the night, you must call to the nurse and bid her still it.

Watch. How if the nurse be asleep and will not hear us?

70 *Dogberry.* Why then, depart in peace and let the child wake her with crying; for the ewe that will not hear her lamb when it baes will never answer a calf when he bleats.

Verges. 'Tis very true.

75 *Dogberry.* This is the end of the charge: you, constable, are to present the Prince's own person. If you meet the Prince in the night, you may stay him.

Verges. Nay, by'r lady, that I think 'a cannot.

Dogberry. Five shillings to one on't, with any man
80 that knows the statutes, he may stay him! Marry, not without the Prince be willing; for indeed the watch ought to offend no man, and it is an offense to stay a man against his will.

Verges. By'r lady, I think it be so.

Dogberry. Ha, ah, ha! Well, masters, good night. And   85
there be any matter of weight chances, call up me.
Keep your fellows' counsels and your own, and
good night. Come, neighbor.

Watch. Well, masters, we hear our charge. Let us go
sit here upon the church bench till two, and then   90
all to bed.

Dogberry. One word more, honest neighbors. I pray
you watch about Signior Leonato's door; for the
wedding being there tomorrow, there is a great coil°
tonight. Adieu. Be vigitant, I beseech you.   95
          Exeunt [Dogberry and Verges].

          Enter Borachio and Conrade.

Borachio. What, Conrade!

Watch. [Aside] Peace! Stir not!

Borachio. Conrade, I say!

Conrade. Here, man. I am at thy elbow.

Borachio. Mass,° and my elbow itched; I thought there   100
would a scab° follow.

Conrade. I will owe thee an answer for that; and now
forward with thy tale.

Borachio. Stand thee close then under this penthouse,°
for it drizzles rain, and I will, like a true drunkard,°   105
utter all to thee.

Watch [Aside] Some treason, masters; yet stand close.

Borachio. Therefore know I have earned of Don John
a thousand ducats.

Conrade. Is it possible that any villainy should be so   110
dear?

94 *coil* to-do, turmoil   100 *Mass* (an interjection, from "by the
Mass")   101 *scab* (1) crust over a wound (2) contemptible person
104 *penthouse* shed, lean-to   105 *drunkard* (his name is based on
the Spanish *borracho,* "drunkard")

Borachio. Thou shouldst rather ask if it were possible any villainy should be so rich; for when rich
villains have need of poor ones, poor ones may
115   make what price they will.

Conrade. I wonder at it.

Borachio. That shows thou art unconfirmed.° Thou
knowest that the fashion of a doublet, or a hat, or
a cloak, is nothing to a man.°

120 *Conrade.* Yes, it is apparel.

Borachio. I mean the fashion.

Conrade. Yes, the fashion is the fashion.

Borachio. Tush! I may as well say the fool's the fool.
But seest thou not what a deformed thief this fash-
125   ion is?

Watch [*Aside*] I know that Deformed; 'a has been a
vile thief this seven year; 'a goes up and down like
a gentleman. I remember his name.

Borachio. Didst thou not hear somebody?

130 *Conrade.* No; 'twas the vane on the house.

Borachio. Seest thou not, I say, what a deformed thief
this fashion is? How giddily 'a turns about all the
hotbloods between fourteen and five-and-thirty?
Sometimes fashioning them like Pharaoh's soldiers
135   in the reechy° painting, sometime like god Bel's
priests° in the old church window, sometime like
the shaven Hercules in the smirched worm-eaten
tapestry, where his codpiece° seems as massy as his
club?

140 *Conrade.* All this I see; and I see that the fashion
wears out more apparel than the man. But art not
thou thyself giddy with the fashion too, that thou

---

117 *unconfirmed* innocent   119 *is nothing to a man* i.e., fails to
reveal his actual character   135 *reechy* grimy, filthy   135–36 *god
Bel's priests* (from the Apocrypha)   138 *codpiece* (decorative
pouch at the fly of a sixteenth-century man's breeches)

hast shifted out of thy tale into telling me of the
fashion?

Borachio. Not so neither. But know that I have tonight 145
wooed Margaret, the Lady Hero's gentlewoman, by
the name of Hero. She leans me out at her mistress'
chamber window, bids me a thousand times good
night. I tell this tale vilely—I should first tell thee
how the Prince, Claudio, and my master, planted 150
and placed and possessed° by my master Don John,
saw afar off in the orchard this amiable encounter.

Conrade. And thought they Margaret was Hero?

Borachio. Two of them did, the Prince and Claudio;
but the devil my master knew she was Margaret; 155
and partly by his oaths, which first possessed them,
partly by the dark night, which did deceive them,
but chiefly by my villainy, which did confirm any
slander that Don John had made, away went Claudio enraged; swore he would meet her, as he was 160
appointed, next morning at the temple, and there,
before the whole congregation, shame her with
what he saw o'ernight and send her home again
without a husband.

First Watch. We charge you in the Prince's name 165
stand!

Second Watch. Call up the right Master Constable.
We have here recovered the most dangerous piece
of lechery that ever was known in the commonwealth. 170

First Watch. And one Deformed is one of them; I
know him; 'a wears a lock.°

Conrade. Masters, masters—

Second Watch. You'll be made bring Deformed forth,
I warrant you. 175

---

151 *possessed* informed, deluded   172 *lock* lovelock, curl of hair
hanging by the ear

Conrade. Masters, never speak; we charge you let us obey you to go with us.°

Borachio. We are like to prove a goodly commodity, being taken up of these men's bills.°

180 *Conrade.* A commodity in question,° I warrant you. Come, we'll obey you.   *Exeunt.*

[Scene IV. *Leonato's house.*]

Enter Hero, and Margaret, and Ursula.

Hero. Good Ursula, wake my cousin Beatrice and desire her to rise.

Ursula. I will, lady.

Hero. And bid her come hither.

5 *Ursula.* Well.   [*Exit.*]

Margaret. Troth, I think your other rabato° were better.

Hero. No, pray thee, good Meg, I'll wear this.

Margaret. By my troth, 's not so good, and I warrant
10   your cousin will say so.

Hero. My cousin's a fool, and thou art another. I'll wear none but this.

Margaret. I like the new tire° within° excellently, if the hair were a thought browner; and your gown's

176–77 *Masters . . . with us* (Conrade is mocking the language of the Second Watch; he means, "Say no more, we will go along with you")   178–79 *We are . . . bills* (Borachio continues the mockery with a series of puns: *commodity* [1] merchandise [2] profit; *taken up* [1] arrested [2] bought on credit; *bills* [1] pikes [2] bonds or sureties)   180 *in question* (1) subject to judicial examination (2) of doubtful value   III.iv.6 *rabato* ruff   13 *tire* headdress   13 *within* in the next room

a most rare fashion, i' faith. I saw the Duchess of 15
Milan's gown that they praise so.

Hero. O, that exceeds, they say.

Margaret. By my troth, 's but a nightgown° in respect
of yours—cloth o' gold and cuts,° and laced with
silver, set with pearls, down sleeves, side-sleeves,° 20
and skirts, round underborne with a bluish tinsel.
But for a fine, quaint,° graceful, and excellent fashion, yours is worth ten on't.

Hero. God give me joy to wear it, for my heart is exceeding heavy. 25

Margaret. 'Twill be heavier soon by the weight of a
man.

Hero. Fie upon thee! Art not ashamed?

Margaret. Of what, lady? Of speaking honorably? Is
not marriage honorable in a beggar? Is not your 30
lord honorable without marriage? I think you would
have me say, "saving your reverence, a husband."
And bad thinking do not wrest true speaking, I'll
offend nobody. Is there any harm in "the heavier
for a husband"? None, I think, and it be the right 35
husband and the right wife; otherwise 'tis light,°
and not heavy. Ask my Lady Beatrice else. Here
she comes.

Enter Beatrice.

Hero. Good morrow, coz.

Beatrice. Good morrow, sweet Hero. 40

Hero. Why, how now? Do you speak in the sick tune?

Beatrice. I am out of all other tune, methinks.

---

18 *nightgown* dressing gown   19 *cuts* slashes to show rich fabric
underneath   20 *down sleeves, side-sleeves* long sleeves covering the
arms, open sleeves hanging from the shoulder   22 *quaint* pretty,
dainty   36 *light* (pun on "wanton")

Margaret. Clap's into° "Light o' love." That goes
without a burden.° Do you sing it, and I'll dance it.

45 *Beatrice.* Ye light o' love with your heels!° Then, if
your husband have stables enough, you'll see he
shall lack no barns.°

Margaret. O illegitimate construction! I scorn that with
my heels.

50 *Beatrice.* 'Tis almost five o'clock, cousin; 'tis time you
were ready. By my troth, I am exceeding ill.
Heigh-ho!

Margaret. For a hawk, a horse, or a husband?

Beatrice. For the letter that begins them all, *H*.°

55 *Margaret.* Well, and you be not turned Turk,° there's
no more sailing by the star.

Beatrice. What means the fool, trow?°

Margaret. Nothing I; but God send everyone their
heart's desire!

60 *Hero.* These gloves the Count sent me, they are an
excellent perfume.

Beatrice. I am stuffed,° cousin; I cannot smell.

Margaret. A maid, and stuffed!° There's goodly catch-
ing of cold.

65 *Beatrice.* O, God help me! God help me! How long
have you professed apprehension?°

Margaret. Ever since you left it. Doth not my wit become me rarely?

Beatrice. It is not seen enough. You should wear it in
70 your cap. By my troth, I am sick.

Margaret. Get you some of this distilled *Carduus*

43 *Clap's into* let us sing   44 *burden* bass part (with pun on "the
heavier for a husband")   45 *Ye . . . your heels* (sexual innuendo)
47 *barns* (pun on "bairns," children)   54 *H* ("ache" was pronounced "aitch")   55 *turned Turk* completely changed   57 *trow*
I wonder   62 *I am stuffed* I have a head cold   63 *stuffed* filled (as
with a child)   66 *apprehension* wit

Benedictus° and lay it to your heart. It is the only
thing for a qualm.°

Hero. There thou prick'st her with a thistle.

Beatrice. Benedictus? Why *Benedictus?* You have   75
some moral° in this *Benedictus.*

Margaret. Moral? No, by my troth, I have no moral
meaning. I meant plain holy thistle. You may think
perchance that I think you are in love. Nay, by'r
lady, I am not such a fool to think what I list;° nor   80
I list not to think what I can; nor indeed I cannot
think, if I would think my heart out of thinking,
that you are in love, or that you will be in love, or
that you can be in love. Yet Benedick was such
another, and now is he become a man. He swore   85
he would never marry; and yet now in despite of
his heart he eats his meat without grudging.° And
how you may be converted I know not; but methinks you look with your eyes as other women do.

Beatrice. What pace is this that thy tongue keeps?   90

Margaret. Not a false gallop.

Enter Ursula.

Ursula. Madam, withdraw. The Prince, the Count,
Signior Benedick, Don John, and all the gallants of
the town are come to fetch you to church.

Hero. Help to dress me, good coz, good Meg, good   95
Ursula.   [*Exeunt.*]

[Scene V. *Another room in Leonato's house.*]

Enter Leonato and the Constable [*Dogberry*], *and
the Headborough* [*Verges*].

71–72 *Carduus Benedictus* blessed thistle, a medicinal herb   73
qualm sensation of sickness   76 *moral* special meaning   80 *list*
please   87 *he eats his meat without grudging* he finds that he can
still eat

Leonato. What would you with me, honest neighbor?

Dogberry. Marry, sir, I would have some confidence
with you that decerns you nearly.

Leonato. Brief, I pray you, for you see it is a busy
5   time with me.

Dogberry. Marry, this it is, sir.

Verges. Yes, in truth it is, sir.

Leonato. What is it, my good friends?

Dogberry. Goodman Verges, sir, speaks a little off the
10   matter—an old man, sir, and his wits are not so
blunt as, God help, I would desire they were; but,
in faith, honest as the skin between his brows.

Verges. Yes, I thank God I am as honest as any man
living that is an old man and no honester than I.

15 *Dogberry.* Comparisons are odorous; Palabras,°
neighbor Verges.

Leonato. Neighbors, you are tedious.

Dogberry. It pleases your worship to say so, but we
are the poor Duke's officers; but truly, for mine
20   own part, if I were as tedious as a king, I could find
in my heart to bestow it all of your worship.

Leonato. All thy tediousness on me, ah?

Dogberry. Yea, and 'twere a thousand pound more
than 'tis; for I hear as good exclamation on your
25   worship as of any man in the city, and though I be
but a poor man, I am glad to hear it.

Verges. And so am I.

Leonato. I would fain know what you have to say.

Verges. Marry, sir, our watch tonight, excepting your
30   worship's presence, ha' ta'en a couple of as arrant
knaves as any in Messina.

III.v.15 *Palabras* (for Spanish *pocas palabras,* few words)

Dogberry. A good old man, sir; he will be talking. As
they say, "When the age is in, the wit is out." God
help us! It is a world to see! Well said, i' faith,
neighbor Verges. Well, God's a good man. And   35
two men ride of a horse, one must ride behind. An
honest soul, i' faith, sir, by my troth he is, as ever
broke bread; but God is to be worshiped; all men
are not alike, alas, good neighbor!

Leonato. Indeed, neighbor, he comes too short of you. 40

Dogberry. Gifts that God gives.

Leonato. I must leave you.

Dogberry. One word, sir. Our watch, sir, have indeed
comprehended two aspicious persons, and we would
have them this morning examined before your wor-   45
ship.

Leonato. Take their examination yourself and bring
it me; I am now in great haste, as it may appear
unto you.

Dogberry. It shall be suffigance.   50

Leonato. Drink some wine ere you go. Fare you well.

[Enter a Messenger.]

Messenger. My lord, they stay for you to give your
daughter to her husband.

Leonato. I'll wait upon them. I am ready.
                              Exit [Leonato,
                              with Messenger].

Dogberry. Go, good partner, go get you to Francis   55
Seacole; bid him bring his pen and inkhorn to the
jail. We are now to examination these men.

Verges. And we must do it wisely.

Dogberry. We will spare for no wit, I warrant you;
here's that shall drive some of them to a non-come.° 60
Only get the learned writer to set down our excom-
munication, and meet me at the jail.   *[Exeunt.]*

  60 *non-come* non compos mentis

[ACT IV

Scene I. *A church.*]

Enter Prince [Don Pedro], [Don John the] Bastard, Leonato, Friar [Francis], Claudio, Benedick, Hero, and Beatrice [and Attendants].

Leonato. Come, Friar Francis, be brief. Only to the plain form of marriage, and you shall recount their particular° duties afterwards.

5 *Friar.* You come hither, my lord, to marry this lady?

Claudio. No.

Leonato. To be married to her; Friar, you come to marry her.

Friar. Lady, you come hither to be married to this count?

10 *Hero.* I do.

Friar. If either of you know any inward impediment why you should not be conjoined, I charge you on your souls to utter it.

Claudio. Know you any, Hero?

15 *Hero.* None, my lord.

IV.i.3 *particular* personal

Friar. Know you any, Count?

Leonato. I dare make his answer, none.

Claudio. O, what men dare do! What men may do!
  What men daily do, not knowing what they do!

Benedick. How now? Interjections? Why then, some   20
  be of° laughing, as, ah, ha, he!°

Claudio. Stand thee by,° friar. Father, by your leave,
  Will you with free and unconstrainèd soul
  Give me this maid your daughter?

Leonato. As freely, son, as God did give her me.   25

Claudio. And what have I to give you back whose worth
  May counterpoise this rich and precious gift?

Don Pedro. Nothing, unless you render her again.

Claudio. Sweet Prince, you learn me noble thankfulness.
  There, Leonato, take her back again.   30
  Give not this rotten orange to your friend.
  She's but the sign and semblance of her honor.
  Behold how like a maid she blushes here!
  O, what authority and show of truth
  Can cunning sin cover itself withal!   35
  Comes not that blood, as modest evidence,
  To witness simple virtue? Would you not swear,
  All you that see her, that she were a maid,
  By these exterior shows? But she is none.
  She knows the heat of a luxurious° bed;   40
  [Her blush is guiltiness, not modesty.]

Leonato. What do you mean, my lord?

Claudio.   Not to be married,
  Not to knit my soul to an approvèd° wanton.

Leonato. Dear my lord, if you, in your own proof,°

20–21 *some be of* some are concerned with   21 *ah, ha, he!* (examples of interjections)   22 *Stand thee by* stand aside   40 *luxurious* lustful   43 *approvèd* tested   44 *proof* experience

45 Have vanquished the resistance of her youth
And made defeat of her virginity—

Claudio. I know what you would say: if I have known°
her,
You will say she did embrace me as a husband,
And so extenuate the 'forehand sin.
50 No, Leonato,
I never tempted her with word too large,
But, as a brother to his sister, showed
Bashful sincerity and comely love.

Hero. And seemed I ever otherwise to you?

55 *Claudio.* Out on thee, seeming! I will write against it.
You seem to me as Dian in her orb,
As chaste as is the bud ere it be blown;°
But you are more intemperate in your blood°
Than Venus, or those pamp'red animals
60 That rage in savage sensuality.

Hero. Is my lord well that he doth speak so wide?°

Leonato. Sweet Prince, why speak not you?

Don Pedro.   What should I speak?
I stand dishonored that have gone about
To link my dear friend to a common stale.°

65 *Leonato.* Are these things spoken, or do I but dream?

Don John. Sir, they are spoken, and these things are
true.

Benedick. This looks not like a nuptial.

Hero.   "True," O God!

Claudio. Leonato, stand I here?
Is this the Prince? Is this the Prince's brother?
70 Is this face Hero's? Are our eyes our own?

Leonato. All this is so. But what of this, my lord?

---

47 *known* had intercourse with   57 *blown* blossomed   58 *blood*
sexual desire   61 *so wide* so far from the truth   64 *stale* prostitute

Claudio. Let me but move one question to your daugh-
      ter;
   And by that fatherly and kindly° power
   That you have in her, bid her answer truly.

Leonato. I charge thee do so, as thou art my child.   75

Hero. O, God defend me! How am I beset!
   What kind of catechizing call you this?

Claudio. To make you answer truly to your name.

Hero. Is it not Hero? Who can blot that name
   With any just reproach?

Claudio.   Marry, that can Hero!   80
   Hero itself can blot out Hero's virtue.
   What man was he talked with you yesternight,
   Out at your window betwixt twelve and one?
   Now, if you are a maid, answer to this.

Hero. I talked with no man at that hour, my lord.   85

Don Pedro. Why, then are you no maiden. Leonato,
   I am sorry you must hear. Upon mine honor
   Myself, my brother, and this grievèd Count
   Did see her, hear her, at that hour last night
   Talk with a ruffian at her chamber window   90
   Who hath indeed, most like a liberal° villain,
   Confessed the vile encounters they have had
   A thousand times in secret.

Don John. Fie, fie! They are not to be named, my
      lord—
   Not to be spoke of;   95
   There is not chastity enough in language
   Without offense to utter them. Thus, pretty lady,
   I am sorry for thy much misgovernment.

Claudio. O Hero! What a Hero hadst thou been
   If half thy outward graces had been placed   100
   About thy thoughts and counsels of thy heart!
   But fare thee well, most foul, most fair, farewell;

73 *kindly* natural   91 *liberal* licentious

Thou pure impiety and impious purity,
For thee I'll lock up all the gates of love,
105   And on my eyelids shall conjecture° hang,
To turn all beauty into thoughts of harm,
And never shall it more be gracious.

Leonato. Hath no man's dagger here a point for me?
              [*Hero swoons.*]

Beatrice. Why, how now, cousin? Wherefore sink you
    down?

Don John. Come, let us go. These things, come thus to
110   light,
Smother her spirits up.
              [*Exeunt Don Pedro, Don John, and Claudio.*]

Benedick. How doth the lady?

Beatrice.   Dead, I think. Help, uncle!
    Hero! Why, Hero! Uncle! Signior Benedick! Friar!

Leonato. O Fate, take not away thy heavy hand!
115   Death is the fairest cover for her shame
That may be wished for.

Beatrice.   How now, cousin Hero?

Friar. Have comfort, lady.

Leonato. Dost thou look up?

Friar.   Yea, wherefore should she not?

Leonato. Wherefore? Why, doth not every earthly thing
120   Cry shame upon her? Could she here deny
The story that is printed in her blood?°
Do not live, Hero; do not ope thine eyes;
For, did I think thou wouldst not quickly die,
Thought I thy spirits were stronger than thy shames,
125   Myself would on the rearward of reproaches
Strike at thy life. Grieved I, I had but one?
Chid I for that at frugal nature's frame?°

105 *conjecture* suspicion   121 *printed in her blood* written in her
blushes   127 *frame* plan

O, one too much by thee! Why had I one?
Why ever wast thou lovely in my eyes?
Why had I not with charitable hand   130
Took up a beggar's issue at my gates,
Who smirchèd thus and mired with infamy,
I might have said, "No part of it is mine;
This shame derives itself from unknown loins"?
But mine, and mine I loved, and mine I praised,   135
And mine that I was proud on, mine so much
That I myself was to myself not mine,
Valuing of her—why she, O, she is fall'n
Into a pit of ink, that the wide sea
Hath drops too few to wash her clean again,   140
And salt too little which may season give°
To her foul tainted flesh!

Benedick.   Sir, sir, be patient.
For my part, I am so attired in wonder,
I know not what to say.

Beatrice. O, on my soul, my cousin is belied!   145

Benedick. Lady, were you her bedfellow last night?

Beatrice. No, truly, not; although, until last night,
I have this twelvemonth been her bedfellow.

Leonato. Confirmed, confirmed! O, that is stronger
     made
Which was before barred up with ribs of iron!   150
Would the two princes lie, and Claudio lie,
Who loved her so that, speaking of her foulness,
Washed it with tears? Hence from her! Let her die.

Friar. Hear me a little;
For I have only been silent so long,   155
And given way unto this course of fortune,
By noting of the lady. I have marked
A thousand blushing apparitions
To start into her face, a thousand innocent shames
In angel whiteness beat away those blushes,   160
And in her eye there hath appeared a fire

141 *season give* act as a preservative

To burn the errors that these princes hold
Against her maiden truth. Call me a fool;
Trust not my reading nor my observations,
165 Which with experimental seal° doth warrant
The tenor° of my book; trust not my age,
My reverence, calling, nor divinity,
If this sweet lady lie not guiltless here
Under some biting error.

Leonato.   Friar, it cannot be.
170 Thou seest that all the grace that she hath left
Is that she will not add to her damnation
A sin of perjury; she not denies it.
Why seek'st thou then to cover with excuse
That which appears in proper nakedness?

175 *Friar.* Lady, what man is he you are accused of?

Hero. They know that do accuse me; I know none.
If I know more of any man alive
Than that which maiden modesty doth warrant,
Let all my sins lack mercy! O my father,
180 Prove you that any man with me conversed
At hours unmeet, or that I yesternight
Maintained the change°of words with any creature,
Refuse me, hate me, torture me to death!

Friar. There is some strange misprision° in the princes.

185 *Benedick.* Two of them have the very bent° of honor;
And if their wisdoms be misled in this,
The practice° of it lives in John the bastard,
Whose spirits toil in frame of villainies.

Leonato. I know not. If they speak but truth of her,
190 These hands shall tear her. If they wrong her honor,
The proudest of them shall well hear of it.
Time hath not yet so dried this blood of mine,
Nor age so eat up my invention,°

165 *experimental seal* seal of experience   166 *tenor* purport   182
maintained the change held exchange   184 *misprision* mistaking
185 *bent* shape (or perhaps "inclination")   187 *practice* scheming
193 *invention* inventiveness

Nor fortune made such havoc of my means,
Nor my bad life reft me so much of friends,   *195*
But they shall find awaked in such a kind
Both strength of limb and policy of mind,
Ability in means, and choice of friends,
To quit° me of them throughly.

Friar.   Pause awhile
And let my counsel sway you in this case.   *200*
Your daughter here the princes left for dead.
Let her awhile be secretly kept in,
And publish it that she is dead indeed;
Maintain a mourning ostentation,°
And on your family's old monument   *205*
Hang mournful epitaphs, and do all rites
That appertain unto a burial.

Leonato. What shall become of this? What will this do?

Friar. Marry, this well carried shall on her behalf
Change slander to remorse; that is some good.   *210*
But not for that dream I on this strange course,
But on this travail look for greater birth.
She dying, as it must be so maintained,
Upon the instant that she was accused,
Shall be lamented, pitied, and excused   *215*
Of every hearer. For it so falls out
That what we have we prize not to the worth
Whiles we enjoy it; but being lacked and lost,
Why, then we rack° the value, then we find
The virtue that possession would not show us   *220*
Whiles it was ours. So will it fare with Claudio.
When he shall hear she died upon his words,
Th' idea of her life shall sweetly creep
Into his study of imagination,°
And every lovely organ° of her life   *225*
Shall come appareled in more precious habit,°
More moving, delicate, and full of life,

---

199 *quit* revenge   204 *Maintain a mourning ostentation* perform the
outward show of mourning   219 *rack* stretch   224 *study of imagination* meditation, musing   225 *organ* physical feature   226 *habit* dress

Into the eye and prospect of his soul
Than when she lived indeed. Then shall he mourn,
230　If ever love had interest in his liver,°
And wish he had not so accusèd her,
No, though he thought his accusation true.
Let this be so, and doubt not but success°
Will fashion the event° in better shape
235　Than I can lay it down in likelihood.
But if all aim, but this, be leveled false,°
The supposition of the lady's death
Will quench the wonder of her infamy;
And if it sort° not well, you may conceal her,
240　As best befits her wounded reputation,
In some reclusive and religious life,
Out of all eyes, tongues, minds, and injuries.

Benedick. Signior Leonato, let the friar advise you;
And though you know my inwardness° and love
245　Is very much unto the Prince and Claudio,
Yet, by mine honor, I will deal in this
As secretly and justly as your soul
Should with your body.

Leonato.　　　　　　　Being that I flow in grief,
The smallest twine may lead me.

250　*Friar.* 'Tis well consented. Presently away;
For to strange sores strangely they strain the cure.
Come, lady, die to live. This wedding day
Perhaps is but prolonged. Have patience and
endure.
　　　　　Exit [with all but Beatrice and Benedick].

Benedick. Lady Beatrice, have you wept all this while?

255　*Beatrice.* Yea, and I will weep a while longer.

Benedick. I will not desire that.

---

230 *liver* (supposed seat of love)　233 *success* what follows　234
event outcome　236 *But if . . . false* but if all conjecture, except this
(i.e., the mere supposition of Hero's death), be aimed (*leveled*)
falsely　239 *sort* turn out　244 *inwardness* most intimate feelings

Beatrice. You have no reason. I do it freely.

Benedick. Surely I do believe your fair cousin is
  wronged.

Beatrice. Ah, how much might the man deserve of me   *260*
  that would right her!

Benedick. Is there any way to show such friendship?

Beatrice. A very even° way, but no such friend.

Benedick. May a man do it?

Beatrice. It is a man's office, but not yours.   *265*

Benedick. I do love nothing in the world so well as you.
  Is not that strange?

Beatrice. As strange as the thing I know not. It were as
  possible for me to say I loved nothing so well as you.
  But believe me not; and yet I lie not. I confess noth-   *275*
  ing, nor I deny nothing. I am sorry for my cousin.

Benedick. By my sword, Beatrice, thou lovest me.

Beatrice. Do not swear and eat it.

Benedick. I will swear by it that you love me, and I
  will make him eat it that says I love not you.   *270*

Beatrice. Will you not eat your word?

Benedick. With no sauce that can be devised to it. I
  protest° I love thee.

Beatrice. Why then, God forgive me!

Benedick. What offense, sweet Beatrice?   *280*

Beatrice. You have stayed me in a happy hour.° I was
  about to protest I loved you.

Benedick. And do it with all thy heart.

Beatrice. I love you with so much of my heart that none
  is left to protest.   *285*

263 *even* direct   278 *protest* avow   281 *in a happy hour* just in
time

Benedick. Come, bid me do anything for thee.

Beatrice. Kill Claudio.

Benedick. Ha! Not for the wide world!

Beatrice. You kill me to deny it. Farewell.

290 *Benedick.* Tarry, sweet Beatrice.   [*He holds her.*]

Beatrice. I am gone, though I am here; there is no love
in you. Nay, I pray you let me go!

Benedick. Beatrice—

Beatrice. In faith, I will go!

295 *Benedick.* We'll be friends first.   [*He lets her go.*]

Beatrice. You dare easier be friends with me than fight
with mine enemy.

Benedick. Is Claudio thine enemy?

Beatrice. Is 'a not approved in the height a villain, that
300 hath slandered, scorned, dishonored my kinswoman?
O that I were a man! What, bear her in hand° until
they come to take hands; and then, with public
accusation, uncovered slander, unmitigated rancor—
O God, that I were a man! I would eat his heart in
305 the market place!

Benedick. Hear me, Beatrice—

Beatrice. Talk with a man out at a window! A proper
saying!

Benedick. Nay, but Beatrice—

310 *Beatrice.* Sweet Hero, she is wronged, she is sland'red,
she is undone.

Benedick. Beat—

Beatrice. Princes and counties! Surely, a princely testi-
mony, a goodly count, Count Comfect;° a sweet gal-
315 lant surely! O that I were a man for his sake! Or that

301 *bear her in hand* fool her   314 *Comfect* sugar candy

I had any friend would be a man for my sake! But
manhood is melted into cursies,° valor into compliment, and men are only turned into tongue, and trim
ones too. He is now as valiant as Hercules that only
tells a lie, and swears it. I cannot be a man with   320
wishing; therefore I will die a woman with grieving.

Benedick. Tarry, good Beatrice. By this hand, I love
thee.

Beatrice. Use it for my love some other way than
swearing by it.   325

Benedick. Think you in your soul the Count Claudio
hath wronged Hero?

Beatrice. Yea, as sure as I have a thought or a soul.

Benedick. Enough, I am engaged. I will challenge him.
I will kiss your hand, and so I leave you. By this   330
hand, Claudio shall render me a dear account. As
you hear of me, so think of me. Go comfort your
cousin. I must say she is dead. And so farewell.

                                        [*Exeunt.*]

[Scene II. *A prison.*]

*Enter the Constables [Dogberry and Verges] and
the Town Clerk [Sexton] in gowns, Borachio,
[Conrade, and Watch].*

Dogberry. Is our whole dissembly appeared?

Verges. O, a stool and a cushion for the sexton.

Sexton. Which be the malefactors?

Dogberry. Marry, that am I and my partner.

317 *cursies* curtsies

5   *Verges.* Nay, that's certain. We have the exhibition to
      examine.

      Sexton. But which are the offenders that are to be ex-
      amined? Let them come before Master Constable.

      Dogberry. Yea, marry, let them come before me. What
10   is your name, friend?

      Borachio. Borachio.

      Dogberry. Pray write down Borachio. Yours, sirrah?°

      Conrade. I am a gentleman, sir, and my name is Con-
      rade.

15 *Dogberry.* Write down Master Gentleman Conrade.
      Masters, do you serve God?

      Both. Yea, sir, we hope.

      Dogberry. Write down that they hope they serve God;
      and write God first, for God defend but God should
20   go before such villains! Masters, it is proved already
      that you are little better than false knaves, and it
      will go near to be thought so shortly. How answer
      you for yourselves?

      Conrade. Marry, sir, we say we are none.

25 *Dogberry.* A marvelous witty fellow, I assure you; but
      I will go about with him.° Come you hither, sirrah;
      a word in your ear. Sir, I say to you, it is thought
      you are false knaves.

      Borachio. Sir, I say to you we are none.°

30 *Dogberry.* Well, stand aside. 'Fore God, they are both
      in a tale.° Have you writ down that they are none?

      Sexton. Master Constable, you go not the way to ex-
      amine. You must call forth the watch that are their
      accusers.

IV.ii.12 *sirrah* (term of address used to an inferior)   26 *go about
with him* get the better of him   29 *none* (apparently pronounced the
same as "known," and so taken by Dogberry in his next speech)
30–31 *they are both in a tale* their stories agree

Dogberry. Yea, marry, that's the eftest° way. Let the   35
watch come forth. Masters, I charge you in the
Prince's name, accuse these men.

First Watch. This man said, sir, that Don John the
Prince's brother was a villain.

Dogberry. Write down Prince John a villain. Why, this   40
is flat perjury, to call a prince's brother villain.

Borachio. Master Constable!

Dogberry. Pray thee, fellow, peace. I do not like thy
look, I promise thee.

Sexton. What heard you him say else?   45

Second Watch. Marry, that he had received a thousand
ducats of Don John for accusing the Lady Hero
wrongfully.

Dogberry. Flat burglary as ever was committed.

Verges. Yea, by mass, that it is.   50

Sexton. What else, fellow?

First Watch. And that Count Claudio did mean, upon
his words, to disgrace Hero before the whole assembly, and not marry her.

Dogberry. O villain! Thou wilt be condemned into   55
everlasting redemption for this.

Sexton. What else?

Watch. This is all.

Sexton. And this is more, masters, than you can deny.   60
Prince John is this morning secretly stol'n away.
Hero was in this manner accused, in this very manner refused, and upon the grief of this suddenly died.
Master Constable, let these men be bound and
brought to Leonato's. I will go before and show him
their examination.   [*Exit*.]   65

35 *eftest* quickest

Dogberry. [*To the Watch*] Come, let them be opinioned.°

Verges. Let them be in the hands of Coxcomb.°

Dogberry. God's my life, where's the sexton? Let him
70   write down the Prince's officer Coxcomb. Come,
bind them. Thou naughty° varlet!

Conrade. Away! You are an ass, you are an ass.

Dogberry. Dost thou not suspect my place? Dost thou
not suspect my years? O that he were here to write
75   me down an ass! But, masters, remember that I am
an ass. Though it be not written down, yet forget
not that I am an ass. No, thou villain, thou art full
of piety, as shall be proved upon thee by good witness. I am a wise fellow; and which is more, an offi-
80   cer; and which is more, a householder; and which is
more, as pretty a piece of flesh as any is in Messina,
and one that knows the law, go to! And a rich fellow
enough, go to! And a fellow that hath had losses; and
one that hath two gowns and everything handsome
85   about him. Bring him away. O that I had been writ
down an ass!   *Exit* [*with the others*].

66–67 *opinioned* (he means "pinioned")   68 *Coxcomb* (apparently
Verges thinks this is an elegant name for one of the Watch; editors
commonly emend "of Coxcomb" to "off, coxcomb," and give to
Conrade)   71 *naughty* wicked

[ACT V

Scene I. *Before Leonato's house.*]

Enter Leonato and his brother [Antonio].

Antonio. If you go on thus, you will kill yourself,
And 'tis not wisdom thus to second° grief
Against yourself.

Leonato.　　　　　I pray thee cease thy counsel,
Which falls into mine ears as profitless
As water in a sieve. Give not me counsel,　　　　　*5*
Nor let no comforter delight mine ear
But such a one whose wrongs do suit with° mine.
Bring me a father that so loved his child,
Whose joy of her is overwhelmed like mine,
And bid him speak of patience.　　　　　*10*
Measure his woe the length and breadth of mine,
And let it answer every strain° for strain,
As thus for thus, and such a grief for such,
In every lineament, branch, shape, and form.
If such a one will smile and stroke his beard,　　　　　*15*
And sorrow wag,° cry "hem" when he should groan;
Patch grief with proverbs, make misfortune drunk
With candle-wasters;° bring him yet° to me,

V.i.2 *second* assist　　7 *suit with* accord with　12 *strain* quality, trait
16 *wag* wave away　18 *candle-wasters* revelers (?) philosophers (?)
18 *yet* then

109

And I of him will gather patience.
20   But there is no such man. For, brother, men
Can counsel and speak comfort to that grief
Which they themselves not feel; but, tasting it,
Their counsel turns to passion, which before
Would give preceptial medicine° to rage,
25   Fetter strong madness in a silken thread,
Charm ache with air and agony with words.
No, no! 'Tis all men's office to speak patience
To those that wring under the load of sorrow,
But no man's virtue nor sufficiency
30   To be so moral° when he shall endure
The like himself. Therefore give me no counsel;
My griefs cry louder than advertisement.°

Antonio. Therein do men from children nothing differ.

Leonato. I pray thee peace. I will be flesh and blood;
35   For there was never yet philosopher
That could endure the toothache patiently,
However they have writ the style of gods
And made a push at chance and sufferance.°

Antonio. Yet bend not all the harm upon yourself.
40   Make those that do offend you suffer too.

Leonato. There thou speak'st reason. Nay, I will do so.
My soul doth tell me Hero is belied;
And that shall Claudio know; so shall the Prince,
And all of them that thus dishonor her.

Enter Prince [Don Pedro] and Claudio.

45 *Antonio.* Here comes the Prince and Claudio hastily.

Don Pedro. Good den, good den.

Claudio.   Good day to both of you.

Leonato. Hear you, my lords—

Don Pedro.   We have some haste, Leonato.

24 *preceptial medicine* medicine of precepts (cf. line 17: "Patch grief with proverbs") 30 *moral* moralizing 32 *advertisement* counsel 38 *made . . . sufferance* defied mischance and suffering

Leonato. Some haste, my lord! Well, fare you well,
   my lord.
  Are you so hasty now? Well, all is one.

Don Pedro. Nay, do not quarrel with us, good old man.   *50*

Antonio. If he could right himself with quarreling,
  Some of us would lie low.

Claudio.   Who wrongs him?

Leonato. Marry, thou dost wrong me, thou dissembler,
   thou!
  Nay, never lay thy hand upon thy sword;
  I fear thee not.

Claudio.   Marry, beshrew° my hand   *55*
  If it should give your age such cause of fear.
  In faith, my hand meant nothing to my sword.

Leonato. Tush, tusn, man! Never fleer° and jest at me.
  I speak not like a dotard nor a fool,
  As under privilege of age to brag   *60*
  What I have done being young, or what would do,
  Were I not old. Know, Claudio, to thy head,°
  Thou hast so wronged mine innocent child and me
  That I am forced to lay my reverence by
  And, with gray hairs and bruise of many days,   *65*
  Do challenge thee to trial of a man.°
  I say thou hast belied mine innocent child.
  Thy slander hath gone through and through her
   heart,
  And she lies buried with her ancestors;
  O, in a tomb where never scandal slept,   *70*
  Save this of hers, framed° by thy villainy!

Claudio. My villainy?

Leonato.   Thine, Claudio; thine I say.

Don Pedro. You say not right, old man.

Leonato.   My lord, my lord,

55 *beshrew* curse (but not a strong word)   58 *fleer* sneer   62 *head*
face   66 *trial of a man* manly test, i.e., a duel   71 *framed* made

I'll prove it on his body if he dare,
75 Despite his nice fence° and his active practice,
His May of youth and bloom of lustihood.

Claudio. Away! I will not have to do with you.

Leonato. Canst thou so daff° me? Thou hast killed my
child.
If thou kill'st me, boy, thou shalt kill a man.

80 *Antonio.* He shall kill two of us, and men indeed.
But that's no matter; let him kill one first.
Win me and wear me! Let him answer me.
Come, follow me, boy; come, sir boy; come, follow
me.
Sir boy, I'll whip you from your foining° fence!
85 Nay, as I am a gentleman, I will.

Leonato. Brother—

Antonio. Content yourself. God knows I loved my
niece;
And she is dead, slandered to death by villains,
That dare as well answer a man indeed
90 As I dare take a serpent by the tongue.
Boys, apes, braggarts, Jacks,° milksops!

Leonato.   Brother Anthony—

Antonio. Hold you content. What, man! I know them,
yea,
And what they weigh, even to the utmost scruple;°
Scambling,° outfacing, fashionmonging° boys,
95 That lie and cog° and flout, deprave and slander,
Go anticly,° and show outward hideousness,
And speak off half a dozen dang'rous words,
How they might hurt their enemies, if they durst;
And this is all.

Leonato. But, brother Anthony—

---

75 *nice fence* elegant fencing   78 *daff* put off   84 *foining* thrusting
91 *Jacks* (a contemptuous term of no precise meaning)   93 *scruple*
smallest unit   94 *Scambling* brawling   94 *fashionmonging* fashion
following   95 *cog* cheat   96 *anticly* grotesquely dressed

Antonio.   Come, 'tis no matter. 100
 Do not you meddle; let me deal in this.

Don Pedro. Gentlemen both, we will not wake your
 patience.°
 My heart is sorry for your daughter's death.
 But, on my honor, she was charged with nothing
 But what was true, and very full of proof.   105

Leonato. My lord, my lord!

Don Pedro. I will not hear you.

Leonato. No? Come, brother, away! I will be heard!

Antonio. And shall, or some of us will smart for it.
    Exeunt ambo° [*Leonato and Antonio*].

    Enter Benedick.

Don Pedro. See, see! Here comes the man we went to
 seek.   110

Claudio. Now, signior, what news?

Benedick. Good day, my lord.

Don Pedro. Welcome, signior. You are almost come
 to part almost a fray.

Claudio. We had liked to have had our two noses 115
 snapped off with two old men without teeth.

Don Pedro. Leonato and his brother. What think'st
 thou? Had we fought, I doubt° we should have been
 too young for them.

Benedick. In a false quarrel there is no true valor. I 120
 came to seek you both.

Claudio. We have been up and down to seek thee; for
 we are high-proof° melancholy, and would fain
 have it beaten away. Wilt thou use thy wit?

---

102 *wake your patience* arouse your indulgence (heavily ironic)
109 s.d. *ambo* both (Latin)   118 *doubt* suspect   123 *high-proof* in
the highest degree

125 *Benedick.* It is in my scabbard. Shall I draw it?

Don Pedro. Dost thou wear thy wit by thy side?

Claudio. Never any did so, though very many have
been beside their wit. I will bid thee draw, as we do
the minstrels: draw° to pleasure us.

130 *Don Pedro.* As I am an honest man, he looks pale.
Art thou sick, or angry?

Claudio. What, courage, man! What though care killed
a cat, thou hast mettle enough in thee to kill care.

Benedick. Sir, I shall meet your wit in the career° and
135 you charge° it against me. I pray you choose another subject.

Claudio. Nay then, give him another staff. This last
was broke cross.°

Don Pedro. By this light, he changes more and more.
140 I think he be angry indeed.

Claudio. If he be, he knows how to turn his girdle.°

Benedick. Shall I speak a word in your ear?

Claudio. God bless me from a challenge!

Benedick. [*Aside to Claudio*] You are a villain; I jest
145 not; I will make it good how you dare, with what
you dare, and when you dare. Do me right, or I will
protest° your cowardice. You have killed a sweet
lady, and her death shall fall heavy on you. Let me
hear from you.

150 *Claudio.* Well, I will meet you, so I may have good
cheer.

Don Pedro. What, a feast, a feast?

Claudio. I' faith, I thank him; he hath bid me to a

---

129 *draw* i.e., draw not a sword but a fiddle bow   134 *in the career*
headlong   135 *charge* i.e., as in tilting with staves or lances   138
broke cross ineptly broken (by crossing the opponent's shield instead
of striking it headlong)   141 *turn his girdle* challenge me (by
reaching for his dagger?)   147 *protest* proclaim

calf's head and a capon; the which if I do not
carve most curiously,° say my knife's naught. Shall
I not find a woodcock° too?   155

Benedick. Sir, your wit ambles well; it goes easily.

Don Pedro. I'll tell thee how Beatrice praised thy wit
the other day. I said thou hadst a fine wit. "True,"
said she, "a fine little one." "No," said I, "a great
wit." "Right," says she, "a great gross one." "Nay,"   165
said I, "a good wit." "Just," said she, "it hurts nobody." "Nay," said I, "the gentleman is wise."
"Certain," said she, "a wise gentleman." "Nay,"
said I, "he hath the tongues."° "That I believe,"   160
said she, " for he swore a thing to me on Monday
night which he forswore on Tuesday morning;
there's a double tongue; there's two tongues." Thus
did she an hour together transshape° thy particu-
lar virtues. Yet at last she concluded with a sigh,   170
thou wast the prop'rest° man in Italy.

Claudio. For the which she wept heartily and said she
cared not.

Don Pedro. Yea, that she did; but yet, for all that, and
if she did not hate him deadly, she would love him   175
dearly. The old man's daughter told us all.

Claudio. All, all! And moreover, God saw him when
he was hid in the garden.

Don Pedro. But when shall we set the savage bull's
horns on the sensible Benedick's head?   180

Claudio. Yea, and text underneath, "Here dwells
Benedick, the married man"?

Benedick. Fare you well, boy; you know my mind. I
will leave you now to your gossiplike humor; you
break jests as braggards do their blades, which God   185

---

155 *curiously* skillfully   156 *woodcock* stupid bird (Claudio reduces
the duel to a carving up of symbols of stupidity—a calf's head, a
capon, and a woodcock)   165 *hath the tongues* knows foreign lan-
guages   169 *transshape* distort   171 *prop'rest* most handsome

be thanked hurt not. [*To Don Pedro*] My lord, for
your many courtesies I thank you. I must discon-
tinue your company. Your brother the bastard is
fled from Messina. You have among you killed a
190   sweet and innocent lady. For my Lord Lackbeard
there, he and I shall meet; and till then peace be
with him.   [*Exit.*]

Don Pedro. He is in earnest.

Claudio. In most profound earnest; and, I'll warrant
195   you, for the love of Beatrice.

Don Pedro. And hath challenged thee?

Claudio. Most sincerely.

Don Pedro. What a pretty thing man is when he goes
in his doublet and hose and leaves off his wit!

> *Enter Constables* [*Dogberry, Verges, and the*
> *Watch, with*] *Conrade and Borachio.*

200 *Claudio.* He is then a giant to an ape; but then is an
ape a doctor to such a man.°

Don Pedro. But, soft you, let me be! Pluck up, my
heart, and be sad. Did he not say my brother was
fled?

205 *Dogberry.* Come you, sir. If justice cannot tame you,
she shall ne'er weigh more reasons in her balance.
Nay, and you be a cursing hypocrite once, you must
be looked to.

Don Pedro. How now? Two of my brother's men
210   bound? Borachio one.

Claudio. Hearken after° their offense, my lord.

Don Pedro. Officers, what offense have these men
done?

200–01 *He is then . . . a man* i.e., an ape would consider him important, but an ape is actually a scholar (*doctor*) compared to such a
fool   211 *Hearken after* inquire into

Dogberry. Marry, sir, they have committed false report; moreover, they have spoken untruths; sec- 215
ondarily, they are slanders; sixth and lastly, they
have belied a lady; thirdly, they have verified unjust
things; and to conclude, they are lying knaves.

Don Pedro. First, I ask thee what they have done;
thirdly, I ask thee what's their offense; sixth and 220
lastly, why they are committed; and to conclude,
what you lay to their charge.

Claudio. Rightly reasoned, and in his own division;
and, by my troth, there's one meaning well suited.°

Don Pedro. Who have you offended, masters, that you 225
are thus bound° to your answer? This learned constable is too cunning° to be understood. What's
your offense?

Borachio. Sweet Prince, let me go no farther to mine
answer. Do you hear me, and let this count kill me. 230
I have deceived even your very eyes. What your
wisdoms could not discover, these shallow fools
have brought to light, who in the night overheard
me confessing to this man, how Don John your
brother incensed me to slander the Lady Hero; 235
how you were brought into the orchard and saw
me court Margaret in Hero's garments; how you
disgraced her when you should marry her. My
villainy they have upon record, which I had rather
seal with my death than repeat over to my shame. 240
The lady is dead upon mine and my master's false
accusation; and briefly, I desire nothing but the
reward of a villain.

Don Pedro. Runs not this speech like iron through
your blood? 245

Claudio. I have drunk poison whiles he uttered it.

Don Pedro. But did my brother set thee on to this?

---

224 *well suited* well dressed out   226 *bound* arraigned   227 *cunning*
intelligent

Borachio. Yea, and paid me richly for the practice
of it.

250 *Don Pedro.* He is composed and framed of treachery,
And fled he is upon this villainy.

Claudio. Sweet Hero, now thy image doth appear
In the rare semblance that I loved it first.

Dogberry. Come, bring away the plaintiffs. By this
255 time our sexton hath reformed Signior Leonato of
the matter. And, masters, do not forget to specify,
when time and place shall serve, that I am an ass.

Verges. Here, here comes Master Signior Leonato,
and the sexton too.

*Enter Leonato, his brother [Antonio], and the
Sexton.*

260 *Leonato.* Which is the villain? Let me see his eyes,
That, when I note another man like him,
I may avoid him. Which of these is he?

Borachio. If you would know your wronger, look on
me.

Leonato. Art thou the slave that with thy breath hast
killed
Mine innocent child?

265 *Borachio.*   Yea, even I alone.

Leonato. No, not so, villain! Thou beliest thyself.
Here stand a pair of honorable men;
A third is fled, that had a hand in it.
I thank you, princes, for my daughter's death.
270 Record it with your high and worthy deeds.
'Twas bravely done, if you bethink you of it.

Claudio. I know not how to pray your patience;°
Yet I must speak. Choose your revenge yourself;
Impose me to what penance your invention°

272 *pray your patience* ask your forgiveness 274 *invention* imagination

Can lay upon my sin. Yet sinned I not   275
But in mistaking.

Don Pedro.   By my soul, nor I;
And yet, to satisfy this good old man,
I would bend under any heavy weight
That he'll enjoin me to.

Leonato. I cannot bid you bid my daughter live;   280
That were impossible; but I pray you both,
Possess° the people in Messina here
How innocent she died; and if your love
Can labor aught in sad invention,
Hang her an epitaph upon her tomb,   285
And sing it to her bones, sing it tonight.
Tomorrow morning come you to my house;
And since you could not be my son-in-law,
Be yet my nephew. My brother hath a daughter,
Almost the copy of my child that's dead,   290
And she alone is heir to both of us.
Give her the right° you should have giv'n her
     cousin,
And so dies my revenge.

Claudio.   O noble sir!
Your overkindness doth wring tears from me.
I do embrace your offer; and dispose   295
For henceforth of poor Claudio.

Leonato. Tomorrow then I will expect your coming;
Tonight I take my leave. This naughty man
Shall face to face be brought to Margaret,
Who I believe was packed° in all this wrong,   300
Hired to it by your brother.

Borachio.   No, by my soul, she was not;
Nor knew not what she did when she spoke to me;
But always hath been just and virtuous
In anything that I do know by her.

---

282 *Possess* inform   292 *right* (Hero had a right to claim Claudio as
her husband; probably there is also a pun on "rite")   300 *packed*
combined, i.e., an accomplice

305 *Dogberry.* Moreover, sir, which indeed is not under
white and black,° this plaintiff here, the offender,
did call me ass. I beseech you let it be rememb'red
in his punishment. And also the watch heard them
talk of one Deformed; they say he wears a key° in
310 his ear, and a lock hanging by it, and borrows
money in God's name, the which he hath used so
long and never paid that now men grow hard-
hearted and will lend nothing for God's sake. Pray
you examine him upon that point.

315 *Leonato.* I thank thee for thy care and honest pains.

Dogberry. Your worship speaks like a most thankful
and reverent youth, and I praise God for you.

Leonato. There's for thy pains.   [*Gives money.*]

Dogberry. God save the foundation!°

320 *Leonato.* Go, I discharge° thee of thy prisoner, and I
thank thee.

Dogberry. I leave an arrant knave with your worship,
which I beseech your worship to correct yourself,
for the example of others. God keep your worship!
325 I wish your worship well. God restore you to health!
I humbly give you leave to depart; and if a merry
meeting may be wished, God prohibit it! Come,
neighbor.   [*Exeunt Dogberry and Verges.*]

Leonato. Until tomorrow morning, lords, farewell.

Antonio. Farewell, my lords. We look for you tomor-
330 row.

Don Pedro. We will not fail.

Claudio.   Tonight I'll mourn with Hero.
                    [*Exeunt Don Pedro and Claudio.*]

305–06 *not under white and black* not in the official record   309 *key*
ring (but perhaps Dogberry merely assumes that if a man wears a
lock in his hair he must wear a key too)   319 *the foundation* (as if
Leonato were a charitable institution)   320 *discharge* relieve

Leonato. [*To the Watch*] Bring you these fellows on.
   We'll talk with Margaret,
How her acquaintance grew with this lewd° fellow.
                              Exeunt [*separately*].

[Scene II. *Leonato's garden.*]

Enter Benedick and Margaret [*meeting*].

Benedick. Pray thee, sweet Mistress Margaret, deserve
   well at my hands by helping me to the speech of
   Beatrice.

Margaret. Will you then write me a sonnet in praise
   of my beauty?   3

Benedick. In so high a style,° Margaret, that no man
   living shall come over it; for in most comely truth
   thou deservest it.

Margaret. To have no man come over me!° Why, shall
   I always keep belowstairs?°   10

Benedick. Thy wit is as quick as the greyhound's
   mouth; it catches.

Margaret. And yours as blunt as the fencer's foils,
   which hit but hurt not.

Benedick. A most manly wit, Margaret; it will not hurt 15
   a woman. And so, I pray thee call Beatrice. I give
   thee the bucklers.°

Margaret. Give us the swords; we have bucklers of
   our own.

Benedick. If you use them, Margaret, you must put   20

333 *lewd* low   V.ii.6 *style* (pun on "stile," a set of steps for passing
over a fence)   9 *come over me* (the beginning of an interchange of
sexual innuendoes)   10 *keep belowstairs* dwell in the servants'
quarters   16–17 *I give thee the bucklers* I yield

in the pikes° with a vice;° and they are dangerous
weapons for maids.

Margaret. Well, I will call Beatrice to you, who I think
hath legs.   *Exit Margaret.*

25 *Benedick.* And therefore will come.
        [*Sings*]   The god of love,
                            That sits above
                    And knows me, and knows me,
                        How pitiful I deserve—
30 I mean in singing; but in loving, Leander the good
swimmer, Troilus° the first employer of panders,
and a whole book full of these quondam carpetmongers,° whose names yet run smoothly in the
even road of a blank verse—why, they were never
35 so truly turned over and over as my poor self in
love. Marry, I cannot show it in rhyme. I have tried.
I can find out no rhyme to "lady" but "baby," an
innocent rhyme; for "scorn," "horn," a hard rhyme;
for "school," "fool," a babbling rhyme. Very omi-
40 nous endings. No, I was not born under a rhyming
planet, nor I cannot woo in festival terms.

Enter Beatrice.

Sweet Beatrice, wouldst thou come when I called
thee?

Beatrice. Yea, signior, and depart when you bid me.

45 *Benedick.* O, stay but till then!

Beatrice. "Then" is spoken. Fare you well now. And
yet, ere I go, let me go with that I came, which is,
with knowing what hath passed between you and
Claudio.

50 *Benedick.* Only foul words; and thereupon I will kiss
thee.

21 *pikes* spikes in the center of bucklers   21 *vice* screw   30–31
Leander . . . Troilus (legendary lovers; Leander nightly swam the
Hellespont to visit Hero, Troilus was aided in his love for Cressida
by Pandarus)   32–33 *quondam carpetmongers* ancient boudoir
knights

Beatrice. Foul words is but foul wind, and foul wind
is but foul breath, and foul breath is noisome.
Therefore I will depart unkissed.

Benedick. Thou hast frighted the word out of his right   55
sense, so forcible is thy wit. But I must tell thee
plainly, Claudio undergoes my challenge; and either
I must shortly hear from him or I will subscribe
him° a coward. And I pray thee now tell me, for
which of my bad parts didst thou first fall in love   60
with me?

Beatrice. For them all together, which maintained so
politic a state° of evil that they will not admit any
good part to intermingle with them. But for which
of my good parts did you first suffer love for me?   65

Benedick. Suffer love! A good epithet. I do suffer love
indeed, for I love thee against my will.

Beatrice. In spite of your heart, I think. Alas, poor
heart! If you spite it for my sake, I will spite it for
yours, for I will never love that which my friend   70
hates.

Benedick. Thou and I are too wise to woo peaceably.

Beatrice. It appears not in this confession. There's not
one wise man among twenty that will praise himself.

Benedick. An old, an old instance,° Beatrice, that   75
lived in the time of good neighbors. If a man do
not erect in this age his own tomb ere he dies, he
shall live no longer in monument than the bell rings
and the widow weeps.

Beatrice. And how long is that, think you?   80

Benedick. Question: why, an hour in clamor and a
quarter in rheum;° therefore is it most expedient
for the wise, if Don Worm, his conscience, find no
impediment to the contrary, to be the trumpet of

58–59 *subscribe him* write him down   63 *politic a state* well-ordered
a community   75 *instance* example   82 *rheum* tears

85   his own virtues, as I am to myself. So much for
      praising myself, who, I myself will bear witness, is
      praiseworthy. And now tell me, how doth your
      cousin?

Beatrice. Very ill.

90 *Benedick.* And how do you?

Beatrice. Very ill too.

Benedick. Serve God, love me, and mend. There will
    I leave you too, for here comes one in haste.

Enter Ursula.

Ursula. Madam, you must come to your uncle. Yon-
95   der's old coil° at home. It is proved my Lady Hero
      hath been falsely accused, the Prince and Claudio
      mightily abused, and Don John is the author of all,
      who is fled and gone. Will you come presently?

Beatrice. Will you go hear this news, signior?

100 *Benedick.* I will live in thy heart, die in thy lap, and
      be buried in thy eyes; and moreover, I will go with
      thee to thy uncle's.   *Exit [with Beatrice and Ursula].*

[Scene III. *A church.*]

*Enter Claudio, Prince [Don Pedro, Lord,] and
three or four with tapers [followed by Musicians].*

Claudio. Is this the monument of Leonato?

Lord. It is, my lord.

[*Claudio reads from a scroll.*]

95 *old coil* plenty of confusion

Epitaph

Done to death by slanderous tongues
   Was the Hero that here lies;
Death, in guerdon° of her wrongs,   5
   Gives her fame which never dies.
So the life that died with shame
Lives in death with glorious fame.
                [*Hangs up the scroll.*]
Hang thou there upon the tomb,
Praising her when I am dumb.   10

Claudio. Now, music, sound, and sing your solemn
   hymn.

Song.

Pardon, goddess of the night,°
Those that slew thy virgin knight;
For the which, with songs of woe,
Round about her tomb they go.   15
Midnight, assist our moan;
Help us to sigh and groan,
   Heavily, heavily.
Graves, yawn and yield your dead,
Till death be utterèd,   20
   Heavily, heavily.

Claudio. Now unto thy bones good night!
   Yearly will I do this rite.

Don Pedro. Good morrow, masters; put your torches
   out.
   The wolves have preyed, and look, the gentle
      day,   25
Before the wheels of Phoebus,° round about
   Dapples the drowsy east with spots of gray.
Thanks to you all, and leave us. Fare you well.

Claudio. Good morrow, masters; each his several way.

V.iii.5 *guerdon* reward   12 *goddess of the night* Diana, goddess of
the moon and of chastity   26 *wheels of Phoebus* wheels of the sun
god's chariot

Don Pedro. Come, let us hence and put on other
30   weeds,°
          And then to Leonato's we will go.

Claudio. And Hymen° now with luckier issue speeds°
          Than this for whom we rend'red up this woe.

                                              Exeunt.

[Scene IV. *Leonato's house.*]

*Enter Leonato, Benedick, [Beatrice,] Margaret,
Ursula, Old Man [Antonio], Friar [Francis],
                    Hero.*

Friar. Did I not tell you she was innocent?

Leonato. So are the Prince and Claudio, who accused
          her
          Upon the error that you heard debated.
          But Margaret was in some fault for this,
5   Although against her will, as it appears
          In the true course of all the question.°

Antonio. Well, I am glad that all things sorts° so well.

Benedick. And so am I, being else by faith enforced
          To call young Claudio to a reckoning for it.

10   *Leonato.* Well, daughter, and you gentlewomen all,
          Withdraw into a chamber by yourselves,
          And when I send for you, come hither masked.
          The Prince and Claudio promised by this hour
          To visit me. You know your office, brother;
15   You must be father to your brother's daughter,
          And give her to young Claudio.   *Exeunt Ladies.*

Antonio. Which I will do with confirmed° counte-
          nance.

30 *weeds* apparel   32 *Hymen* god of marriage   32 *speeds* succeeds
V.iv.6 *question* investigation   7 *sorts* turn out   17 *confirmed*
steady

Benedick. Friar, I must entreat your pains, I think.

Friar. To do what, signior?

Benedick. To bind me, or undo me—one of them.   20
Signior Leonato, truth it is, good signior,
Your niece regards me with an eye of favor.

Leonato. That eye my daughter lent her; 'tis most true.

Benedick. And I do with an eye of love requite her.

Leonato. The sight whereof I think you had from me,   25
From Claudio, and the Prince. But what's your will?

Benedick. Your answer, sir, is enigmatical.
But, for my will, my will is, your good will
May stand with ours, this day to be conjoined
In the state of honorable marriage;   30
In which, good friar, I shall desire your help.

Leonato. My heart is with your liking.

Friar.   And my help.
Here comes the Prince and Claudio.

*Enter Prince [Don Pedro] and Claudio and two
or three other.*

Don Pedro. Good morrow to this fair assembly.

Leonato. Good morrow, Prince; good morrow, Clau-
dio.   35
We here attend you. Are you yet determined
Today to marry with my brother's daughter?

Claudio. I'll hold my mind, were she an Ethiope.

Leonato. Call her forth, brother. Here's the friar
ready.   [*Exit Antonio.*]

Don Pedro. Good morrow, Benedick. Why, what's the
matter   40
That you have such a February face,
So full of frost, of storm, and cloudiness?

Claudio. I think he thinks upon the savage bull.°
    Tush, fear not, man! We'll tip thy horns with gold,°
45 And all Europa° shall rejoice at thee,
    As once Europa did at lusty Jove
    When he would play the noble beast in love.

Benedick. Bull Jove, sir, had an amiable low,
    And some such strange bull leaped your father's
        cow
50 And got a calf in that same noble feat
    Much like to you, for you have just his bleat.

*Enter [Leonato's] brother [Antonio], Hero,
Beatrice, Margaret, Ursula, [the ladies wearing
masks].*

Claudio. For this I owe you.° Here comes other
    reck'nings.
    Which is the lady I must seize upon?

Antonio. This same is she, and I do give you her.

Claudio. Why then, she's mine. Sweet, let me see your
55   face.

Leonato. No, that you shall not till you take her hand
    Before this friar and swear to marry her.

Claudio. Give me your hand; before this holy friar
    I am your husband if you like of me.

60 *Hero.* And when I lived I was your other wife; [*un-
    masking*]
    And when you loved you were my other husband.

Claudio. Another Hero!

Hero.   Nothing certainer.
    One Hero died defiled; but I do live,
    And surely as I live, I am a maid.

---

43 *savage bull* (refers to I.i.252)   44 *tip thy horns with gold* i.e.,
make your cuckolding something to be proud of   45 *Europa*
Europe (though in the next line the word designates the girl that
Jupiter wooed in the guise of a bull)   52 *I owe you* i.e., I will pay you
back (for calling me a calf and a bastard)

Don Pedro. The former Hero! Hero that is dead!   65

Leonato. She died, my lord, but whiles° her slander
    lived.

Friar. All this amazement can I qualify,°
  When, after that the holy rites are ended,
  I'll tell you largely° of fair Hero's death.
  Meantime let wonder seem familiar,   70
  And to the chapel let us presently.

Benedick. Soft and fair, friar. Which is Beatrice?

Beatrice [*Unmasking*] I answer to that name. What is
    your will?

Benedick. Do not you love me?

Beatrice.   Why, no; no more than reason.

Benedick. Why, then your uncle, and the Prince, and
  Claudio   75
  Have been deceived—they swore you did.

Beatrice. Do not you love me?

Benedick.   Troth, no; no more than reason.

Beatrice. Why, then my cousin, Margaret, and Ursula
  Are much deceived; for they did swear you did.

Benedick. They swore that you were almost sick for
    me.   80

Beatrice. They swore that you were well-nigh dead for
    me.

Benedick. 'Tis no such matter. Then you do not love
    me?

Beatrice. No, truly, but in friendly recompense.

Leonato. Come, cousin, I am sure you love the gen-
    tleman.

Claudio. And I'll be sworn upon't that he loves her;   85
  For here's a paper written in his hand,

66 *but whiles* only while   67 *qualify* abate   69 *largely* in detail

A halting° sonnet of his own pure brain,
Fashioned to Beatrice.

Hero.   And here's another,
Writ in my cousin's hand, stol'n from her pocket,
90 Containing her affection unto Benedick.

Benedick. A miracle! Here's our own hands against our
hearts. Come, I will have thee; but, by this light, I
take thee for pity.

Beatrice. I would not deny you; but, by this good day,
95 I yield upon great persuasion, and partly to save
your life, for I was told you were in a consumption.

Benedick.° Peace! I will stop your mouth. [*Kisses her.*]

Don Pedro. How dost thou, Benedick, the married
man?

100 *Benedick.* I'll tell thee what, Prince: a college of wit-
crackers cannot flout me out of my humor. Dost
thou think I care for a satire or an epigram? No. If
a man will be beaten with brains, 'a shall wear nothing handsome about him. In brief, since I do pur-
105 pose to marry, I will think nothing to any purpose
that the world can say against it; and therefore never
flout at me for what I have said against it; for man
is a giddy thing, and this is my conclusion. For thy
part, Claudio, I did think to have beaten thee; but in
110 that thou art like to be my kinsman, live unbruised,
and love my cousin.

Claudio. I had well hoped thou wouldst have denied
Beatrice, that I might have cudgeled thee out of thy
single life, to make thee a double-dealer,° which out
115 of question thou wilt be if my cousin do not look
exceeding narrowly to thee.

Benedick. Come, come, we are friends. Let's have a

---

87 *halting* limping 97 *Benedick* (both Quarto and Folio assign
this line to Leonato; possibly the original reading is correct, and
Leonato forces Benedick to kiss Beatrice) 114 *double-dealer*
(1) married man (2) unfaithful husband

dance ere we are married, that we may lighten our
own hearts and our wives' heels.

Leonato. We'll have dancing afterward.   120

Benedick. First, of my word; therefore play, music.
Prince, thou art sad; get thee a wife, get thee a wife!
There is no staff more reverend than one tipped with
horn.°

Enter Messenger.

Messenger. My lord, your brother John is ta'en in
flight,   125
And brought with armèd men back to Messina.
Benedick. Think not on him till tomorrow. I'll devise
thee brave punishments for him. Strike up, pipers!
Dance. [*Exeunt.*]

FINIS.

123–24 *with horn* (final reference to the horns of a cuckold)

Textual Note

The present text of *Much Ado About Nothing* is based upon the Quarto edition of the play, published in 1600. The Folio text of 1623 is a slightly edited version of this Quarto.

In I.ii Antonio is designated "Old" in the Quarto, meaning old man. In II.i Antonio's speeches are assigned to "Brother." In IV.ii "Kemp" and "Cowley," the actors intended for the roles, are assigned the speeches for Dogberry and Verges. The present edition regularizes all speech prefixes. All act and scene divisions are bracketed, since (like indications of locale) these are not in the Quarto. Spelling and punctuation have been modernized, and obvious typographical errors have been corrected. The positions of a few stage directions have been slightly altered; necessary directions that are not given in the Quarto are added in brackets. Other substantial departures from the Quarto are listed below, the adopted reading first, in italics, and then the Quarto's reading in roman type. If the adopted reading comes from the Folio, the fact is indicated by [F] following it.

I.i.s.d. [Q has "Innogen his wife," i.e., Leonato's wife, before "Hero"; she does not appear in the play] 1 *Don Pedro* Don Peter 9–10 *Don Pedro* Don Peter 195 *Enter Don Pedro* Enter don Pedro, Iohn the bastard

II.i.s.d. *Hero* his wife, Hero *niece* neece, and a kinsman 84 s.d. *Don John* or dumb Iohn 208 s.d. [Q adds "Iohn and Borachio, and Conrade"]

II.iii.138 *us of* [F] of vs
III.ii.52 *Don Pedro* [F] Bene

IV.ii.s.d. [Q places "Borachio" immediately after "Constables"]

V.iii.10 *dumb* [F] dead 22 *Claudio* Lo[rd]

V.iv.54 *Antonio* Leo 97 *Benedick* Leon

132

A Note on the Source of
"Much Ado About Nothing"

Much Ado About Nothing combines two plots, the Hero-Claudio tragicomic one and the Beatrice-Benedick comic one. Shakespeare himself seems to have hit on the idea of joining the two, though if he knew of an earlier work in which they had already been combined, he surely would not have scrupled to follow suit.

The gist of the Hero-Claudio plot—a girl is said to be false and her fiancé is so deceived that he denounces her, though later they are reconciled—is ancient. It is also the basis of a series of stories popular in the sixteenth century. It can scarcely be doubted that Shakespeare knew it in the versions of Ariosto (*Orlando Furioso* was translated by Sir John Harington and plundered by Edmund Spenser) and Bandello (the *Novelle* were translated into French by Belleforest). Quite possibly Shakespeare was acquainted with a number of other versions. Shakespeare's own addition of Dogberry and Verges, for which at best he had only bare hints, gives this Hero-Claudio plot most of its vitality.

The comic intrigue of Beatrice and Benedick is scarcely a plot, and it would be foolish to attempt to isolate a source for it. Sixteenth-century literature offers numerous ladies and gentlemen who wittily scorn each other. In the English drama before Shakespeare, John Lyly had made something of a specialty of such combats. There are, moreover, non-dramatic works (Lyly is again relevant) that may also have given Shakespeare hints. Possibly a paragraph in Castiglione's *Il Cortegiano* (translated by Sir Thomas Hoby) sparked his imagination:

> I have also seen a most fervent love spring in the heart of a woman toward one that seemed at first not to bear him the least affection in the world, only for that they heard say that the opinion of many was that they loved together.

It should be remembered, too, that Beatrice and Benedick are not Shakespeare's first witty, bickering lovers. In *Love's Labor's Lost,* Biron ("not a word with him but a jest") and Rosaline ("a wightly wanton") anticipate Beatrice and Benedick.

Passages from several books that probably influenced *Much Ado* are given in the second volume of Geoffrey Bullough's *Narrative and Dramatic Sources of Shakespeare,* but when one has read *Much Ado* each source seems like Charles Lamb's poor relation: "the most irrelevant thing in nature—a piece of impertinent correspondency."

Commentaries

CHARLES GILDON

The Argument of "Much Ado About Nothing"

The scene lies at Messina in Sicily and in and near the house of Leonato. Don Pedro of Aragon with his favorite Claudio, and Benedick a gay young cavalier of Padua, and Don John the bastard brother of Don Pedro, come to Leonato's, the Governor of Messina. Claudio is in love with Hero, Leonato's daughter, whom Don Pedro obtains for him, and while they wait the wedding day, they consult how to make Benedick and Beatrice, the niece of Leonato, in love with each other, both being gay and easy and averse to love and like great talkers, railing always at each other. However, by letting them overhear their discourse they persuade them that they are in love with each other. In the meantime Don John, the very soul of envy and mischief, contrives how to break the match betwixt Claudio and Hero, and to this purpose, by his engines, Conrade and Borachio, they make Claudio and the Prince believe that Hero is a wanton and put a plausible cheat on them to confirm the suspicion by having Borachio talk to Hero's maid, Margaret, at the chamber window at midnight, as if she were Hero. Convinced by this fal-

From *The Works of Mr. William Shakespear*, 1710.

lacy, Claudio and Don Pedro disgrace her in the church
where he went to marry her, rejecting her, and accusing
her of wantonness with another. Hero swoons away, and,
the priest interposing and joining in the attestation she
makes of her virtue, she is privately conveyed away and
reported dead. The rogue Borachio being taken by the
watch, as he was telling the adventure to his comrade, discovers the villainy and clears Hero; but Don John is fled.
Her innocence being known, her father is satisfied with
Claudio, that he hang verses on her tomb that night and
marry a niece of his the next morning without seeing her
face, which he agrees to and performs, and then it is discovered that it is Hero whom he married and so the play
ends with an account of Don John's being taken.

This fable is as full of absurdities as the writing is full
of beauties: the first I leave to the reader to find out by
the rules I have laid down; the second I shall endeavor
to show and point out some few of the many that are con-
tained in the play. Shakespear indeed had the misfortune
which other of our poets have since had of laying his
scene in a warm climate where the manners of the people
are very different from ours, and yet he has made them
talk and act generally like men of a colder country; *Marriage à la Mode* has the same fault.

This play we must call a comedy, though some of the
incidents and discourses too are more in a tragic strain;
and that of the accusation of Hero is too shocking for
either tragedy or comedy; nor could it have come off in
nature, if we regard the country, without the death of
more than Hero. The imposition on the Prince and Claudio seems very lame, and Claudio's conduct to the woman
he loved highly contrary to the very nature of love, to
expose her in so barbarous a manner and with so little
concern and struggle, and on such weak grounds without
a farther examination into the matter, yet the passions
this produces in the old father make a wonderful amends
for the fault. Besides which there is such a pleasing variety of characters in the play, and those perfectly maintained, as well as distinguished, that you lose the absurdities of the conduct in the excellence of the manners,

sentiments, diction, and topics. Benedick and Beatrice are two sprightly, witty, talkative characters, and, though of the same nature, yet perfectly distinguished, and you have no need to read the names to know who speaks. As they differ from each other, though so near akin, so do they from that of Lucio in *Measure for Measure,* who is likewise a very talkative person; but there is a gross abusiveness, calumny, lying, and lewdness in Lucio, which Benedick is free from. One is a rake's mirth and tattle; the other that of a gentleman and a man of spirit and wit.

The stratagem of the Prince on Benedick and Beatrice is managed with that nicety and address that we are very well pleased with the success and think it very reasonable and just.

The character of Don John the Bastard is admirably distinguished, his manners are well marked, and everywhere convenient or agreeable. Being a sour, melancholy, saturnine, envious, selfish, malicious temper—manners necessary to produce these villainous events they did— these were productive of the catastrophe, for he was not a person brought in to fill up the number only, because without him the fable could not have gone on.

To quote all the comic excellencies of this play would be to transcribe three parts of it. For all that passes betwixt Benedick and Beatrice is admirable. His discourse against love and marriage in the later end of the second act is very pleasant and witty, and that which Beatrice says of wooing, wedding, and repenting. And the aversion that the poet gives Benedick and Beatrice for each other in their discourse heightens the jest of making them in love with one another. Nay, the variety and natural distinction of the vulgar humors of this play are remarkable.

The scenes of this play are something obscure, for you can scarce tell where the place is in the two first acts, though the scenes in them seem pretty entire and unbroken. But those are things we ought not to look much for in Shakespear. But whilst he is out in the dramatic imitation of the fable, he always draws men and women so perfectly that when we read, we can scarce persuade ourselves but that the discourse is real and no fiction.

LEWIS CARROLL

A Letter to Ellen Terry

Now I'm going to put before you a "Hero-ic" puzzle of mine, but please remember I do not ask for your solution of it, as you will persist in believing, if I ask your help in a Shakespeare difficulty, that I am only jesting! However, if you won't attack it yourself, perhaps you would ask Mr. Irving someday how *he* explains it?

My difficulty is this: Why in the world did not Hero (or at any rate Beatrice on her behalf) prove an "alibi" in answer to the charge? It seems certain that she did *not* sleep in her room that night; for how could Margaret venture to open the window and talk from it, with her mistress asleep in the room? It would be sure to wake her. Besides Borachio says, after promising that Margaret shall speak with him out of Hero's chamber window, "I will so fashion the matter that Hero shall be absent." (*How* he could possibly manage any such thing is another difficulty, but I pass over that.) Well then, granting that Hero slept in some other room that night, why didn't she say so? When Claudio asks her: "What man was he talked with you yesternight out at your window betwixt twelve and one?" why doesn't she reply: "I talked with no man at that hour, my lord. Nor was I in my chamber yesternight, but in another, far from it, remote." And this she could, of course, prove by the evidence of the housemaids, who

From *The Story of My Life* by Ellen Terry. 2nd ed. London: Hutchinson and Company, n.d.

must have known that she had occupied another room that night.

But even if Hero might be supposed to be so distracted as not to remember where she had slept the night before, or even whether she had slept *anywhere,* surely *Beatrice* has her wits about her! And when an arrangement was made, by which she was to lose, for one night, her twelve-months' bedfellow, is it conceivable that she didn't know *where* Hero passed the night? Why didn't *she* reply:

> But good my lord sweet Hero slept not there:
> She had another chamber for the nonce.
> 'Twas sure some counterfeit that did present
> Her person at the window, aped her voice,
> Her mien, her manners, and hath thus deceived
> My good Lord Pedro and this company?

With all these excellent materials for proving an "alibi" it is incomprehensible that no one should think of it. If only there had been a barrister present, to cross-examine Beatrice!

"Now, ma'am, attend to me, please, and speak up so that the jury can hear you. Where did you sleep last night? Where did Hero sleep? Will you swear that she slept in her own room? Will you swear that you do not know where she slept?" I feel inclined to quote old Mr. Weller and to say to Beatrice at the end of the play (only I'm afraid it isn't etiquette to speak across the footlights):

"Oh, Samivel, Samivel, vy vornt there a halibi?"

GEORGE BERNARD SHAW

Shakespear's Merry Gentlemen

MUCH ADO ABOUT NOTHING. St. James's Theatre, 16
February 1898.   [26 *February* 1898]

Much Ado is perhaps the most dangerous actor-manager trap in the whole Shakespearean repertory. It is not
a safe play like *The Merchant of Venice* or *As You Like
It,* nor a serious play like *Hamlet.* Its success depends on
the way it is handled in performance; and that, again,
depends on the actor-manager being enough of a critic
to discriminate ruthlessly between the pretension of the
author and his achievement.

The main pretension in *Much Ado* is that Benedick
and Beatrice are exquisitely witty and amusing persons.
They are, of course, nothing of the sort. Benedick's pleas-
antries might pass at a singsong in a public-house parlor;
but a gentleman rash enough to venture on them in even
the very mildest £52-a-year suburban imitation of polite
society today would assuredly never be invited again.
From his first joke, "Were you in doubt, sir, that you
asked her?" to his last, "There is no staff more reverend
than one tipped with horn," he is not a wit, but a blackguard. He is not Shakespear's only failure in that genre.
It took the Bard a long time to grow out of the provincial
conceit that made him so fond of exhibiting his accom-
plishments as a master of gallant badinage. The very
thought of Biron, Mercutio, Gratiano, and Benedick must,
I hope, have covered him with shame in his later years.
Even Hamlet's airy compliments to Ophelia before the
court would make a cabman blush. But at least Shakespear did not value himself on Hamlet's indecent jests as

From *Our Theatres in the Nineties* by George Bernard Shaw. 3 vols.
London: Constable & Co., Ltd., 1932. Reprinted by permission of the
Public Trustee and the Society of Authors.

he evidently did on those of the four merry gentlemen of the earlier plays. When he at last got conviction of sin, and saw this sort of levity in its proper light, he made masterly amends by presenting the blackguard *as* a blackguard in the person of Lucio in *Measure for Measure*. Lucio, as a character study, is worth forty Benedicks and Birons. His obscenity is not only inoffensive, but irresistibly entertaining, because it is drawn with perfect skill, offered at its true value, and given its proper interest, without any complicity of the author in its lewdness. Lucio is much more of a gentleman than Benedick, because he keeps his coarse sallies for coarse people. Meeting one woman, he says humbly, "Gentle and fair: your brother kindly greets you. Not to be weary with you, he's in prison." Meeting another, he hails her sparkingly with "How now? which of your hips has the more profound sciatica?" The one woman is a lay sister, the other a prostitute. Benedick or Mercutio would have cracked their low jokes on the lay sister, and been held up as gentlemen of rare wit and excellent discourse for it. Whenever they approach a woman or an old man, you shiver with apprehension as to what brutality they will come out with.

Precisely the same thing, in the tenderer degree of her sex, is true of Beatrice. In her character of professed wit she has only one subject, and that is the subject which a really witty woman never jests about, because it is too serious a matter to a woman to be made light of without indelicacy. Beatrice jests about it for the sake of the indelicacy. There is only one thing worse than the Elizabethan "merry gentleman," and that is the Elizabethan "merry lady."

Why is it then that we still want to see Benedick and Beatrice, and that our most eminent actors and actresses still want to play them? Before I answer that very simple question let me ask another. Why is it that Da Ponte's "dramma giocosa," entitled *Don Giovanni,* a loathsome story of a coarse, witless, worthless libertine, who kills an old man in a duel and is finally dragged down through a trapdoor to hell by his twaddling ghost, is still, after more than a century, as "immortal" as *Much Ado?* Simply because Mozart clothed it with wonderful music, which turned the worthless words and thoughts of Da Ponte into a magical human drama of moods and transitions of feeling. That is what happened in a smaller way with *Much Ado*. Shakespear shews himself in it a commonplace librettist working on a stolen plot, but a great musician. No matter how poor, coarse, cheap, and obvious the thought may be, the mood is charming, and the music of the words expresses the mood. Paraphrase the encounters of Benedick and Beatrice in the style of a bluebook, carefully preserving every idea they present, and it will become apparent to the most infatuated Shakespearean that they contain at best nothing out of the common in thought or wit, and at worst a good deal of vulgar naughtiness. Paraphrase Goethe, Wagner, or Ibsen in the same way, and you will find original observation, subtle thought, wide comprehension, far-reaching intuition, and serious psychological study in them. Give Shakespear a fairer chance in the comparison by paraphrasing even his best and maturest work, and you will still get nothing more than the platitudes of proverbial philosophy, with a very occasional curiosity in the shape of a rudiment of some modern idea, not followed up. Not until the Shakespearean music is added by replacing the paraphrase with the original lines does the enchantment begin. Then you are in another world at once. When a flower girl tells a coster to hold his jaw, for nobody is listening to him, and he retorts, "Oh, you're there, are you, you beauty?" they reproduce the wit of Beatrice and Benedick exactly. But put it this way: "I wonder that you will still be talking, Signior Benedick: nobody marks you." "What! my dear Lady Disdain, are you yet living?" You are miles away from costerland at once. When I tell you that Benedick and the coster are equally poor in thought, Beatrice and the flower girl equally vulgar in repartee, you reply that I might as well tell you that a nightingale's love is no higher than a cat's. Which is exactly what I do tell you, though the nightingale is the better musician. You will admit, perhaps, that the love of the worst human singer in the world is accompanied by a higher degree of intellectual consciousness than that of the most ravishingly melodious nightingale. Well, in just the same way, there are plenty of quite second-rate writers who are abler thinkers and wits than William, though they are unable to weave his magic into the expression of their thoughts.

It is not easy to knock this into the public head, because comparatively few of Shakespear's admirers are at all conscious that they are listening to music as they hear his phrases turn and his lines fall so fascinatingly and memorably; whilst we all, no matter how stupid we are, can understand his jokes and platitudes, and are flattered when we are told of the subtlety of the wit we have relished, and the profundity of the thought we have fathomed. Englishmen are specially susceptible to this sort of flattery, because intellectual subtlety is not their strong point. In dealing with them you must make them believe that you are appealing to their brains when you are really appealing to their senses and feelings. With Frenchmen the case is reversed: you must make them believe that you are appealing to their senses and feelings when you are really appealing to their brains. The Englishman, slave to every sentimental ideal and dupe of every sensuous art, will have it that his great national poet is a thinker. The Frenchman, enslaved and duped only by systems and calculations, insists on his hero being a sentimentalist and artist. That is why Shakespear is esteemed a mastermind in England and wondered at as a clumsy barbarian in France.

However indiscriminate the public may be in its Shakespear worship, the actor and actress who are to make a success of *Much Ado* must know better. Let them once make the popular mistake of supposing that what they have to do is to bring out the wit of Benedick and Beatrice, and they are lost. Their business in the "merry" passages is to cover poverty of thought and coarseness of innuendo by making the most of the grace and dignity of the diction. The sincere, genuinely dramatic passages will then take care of themselves. Alas! Mr. Alexander and Miss Julia Neilson have made the plunge without waiting for my advice. Miss Neilson, throwing away all her grace and all her music, strives to play the merry lady by dint of conscientious gamboling. Instead of uttering her speeches as exquisitely as possible, she rattles through them, laying an impossible load of archness on every insignificant conjunction, and clipping all the important words until there is no measure or melody left in them. Not even the wedding scene can stop her: after an indignant attitude or two she redoubles her former skittishness. I can only implore her to give up all her deep-laid Beatricisms, to discard the movements of Miss Ellen Terry, the voice of Mrs. Patrick Campbell, and the gaiety of Miss Kitty Loftus, and try the effect of Julia Neilson in all her grave grace taken quite seriously. Mr. Alexander makes the same mistake, though, being more judicious than Miss Neilson, he does not carry it out so disastrously. His merry gentleman is patently a dutiful assumption from beginning to end. He smiles, rackets, and bounds up and down stairs like a quiet man who has just been rated by his wife for habitual dullness before company. It is all hopeless: the charm of Benedick cannot be realized by the spryness of the actor's legs, the flashing of his teeth, or the rattle of his laugh: nothing but the music of the words—above all, not their meaning—can save the part. I wish I could persuade Mr. Alexander that if he were to play the part exactly as he played Guy Domville, it would at once become ten times more fascinating. He should at least take the revelation of Beatrice's supposed love for him with perfect seriousness. The more remorsefully sympathetic Benedick is when she comes to bid him to dinner after he has been gulled into believing she loves him, the more exquisitely ridiculous the scene becomes. It is the audience's turn to laugh then, not Benedick's.

Of all Sir Henry Irving's manifold treasons against Shakespear, the most audacious was his virtually cutting Dogberry out of *Much Ado*. Mr. Alexander does not go so far; but he omits the fifth scene of the third act, upon which the whole effect of the later scenes depends, since it is from it that the audience really gets Dogberry's measure. Dogberry is a capital study of parochial character. Sincerely played, he always comes out as a very real and highly entertaining person. At the St. James's, I grieve to say, he does not carry a moment's conviction: he is a mere mouthpiece for malapropisms, all of which he shouts at the gallery with intense consciousness of their absurdity, and with open anxiety lest they should pass unnoticed.

Surely it is clear, if anything histrionic is clear, that Dogberry's first qualification must be a complete unconsciousness of himself as he appears to others.

Verges, even more dependent than Dogberry on that cut-out scene with Leonato, is almost annihilated by its excision; and it was hardly worth wasting Mr. Esmond on the remainder.

When I have said that neither Benedick nor Beatrice have seen sufficiently through the weakness of Shakespear's merriments to concentrate themselves on the purely artistic qualities of their parts, and that Dogberry is nothing but an excuse for a few laughs, I have made a somewhat heavy deduction from my praises of the revival. But these matters are hardly beyond remedy; and the rest is excellent. Miss Fay Davis's perfect originality contrasts strongly with Miss Neilson's incorrigible imitativeness. Her physical grace is very remarkable; and she creates her part between its few lines, as Hero must if she is to fill up her due place in the drama. Mr. Fred Terry is a most engaging Don Pedro; and Mr. H. B. Irving is a striking Don John, though he is becoming too accomplished an actor to make shift with that single smile which is as well known at the St. James's by this time as the one wig of Mr. Pinero's hero was at "The Wells." Mr. Vernon and Mr. Beveridge are, of course, easily within their powers as Leonato and Antonio; and all the rest come off with credit—even Mr. Loraine, who has not a trace of Claudio in him. The dresses are superb, and the scenery very handsome, though Italy contains so many palaces and chapels that are better than handsome that I liked the opening scenes best. If Mr. Alexander will only make up his mind that the piece is irresistible as poetry, and hopeless as epigrammatic comedy, he need not fear for its success. But if he and Miss Neilson persist in depending on its attempts at wit and gallantry, then it remains to be seen whether the public's sense of duty or its boredom will get the upper hand.

I had intended to deal here with the O.U.D.S. and its performance of *Romeo and Juliet;* but *Much Ado* has carried me too far; so I must postpone Oxford until next week.

DONALD A. STAUFFER

from *Shakespeare's World of Images*

The spirit of the farces, *The Taming of the Shrew* and *The Merry Wives of Windsor,* most nearly parallels the approach to romantic love in *Much Ado About Nothing.* Like them, this play is written with more than a dash of prosaic common sense. Portia's real home had been in the gardens and galleries of Belmont, from which she sallies forth into the world of action like a feminine and effective Don Quixote. But in *Much Ado About Nothing* Shakespeare's sympathy from the beginning lies with the hardheaded and sharp-tongued Benedick and Beatrice. The play constitutes his severest criticism to date of the weaknesses lying in romantic love. He takes as his main plot a highly fanciful story—what could be more romantic than a crucial scene in which a lady swoons into supposed death upon hearing her honor falsely traduced by her lover at the altar? Yet the lady Hero, shadowy and almost silent, is strangely ineffective, the villain is little more than a conventional malcontent, and Shakespeare is satisfied to develop in a few fine touches the weak impulses of his smart young gentleman Claudio.[1]

So full of tricks is fancy, that Claudio in his melodramatic scene of accusation, rails against the "cunning sin"

From *Shakespeare's World of Images* by Donald A. Stauffer. New York: W. W. Norton and Company, Inc., 1949; London: Oxford University Press, 1952. Copyright, 1949, by W. W. Norton and Company, Inc., and reprinted by their permission.

[1] His misliking is as sudden as his liking, and at the first zephyr of suspicion he is quick to note that "beauty is a witch/Against whose charms faith melteth into blood" (II.i.177–78). Benedick sees him as a "poor hurt fowl" that will "now . . . creep into sedges" (II.i.200–01).

and "savage sensuality" of his Hero, who is as modest, chaste, and sincere in reality as he accuses her of being only in "exterior shows." He willfully makes over the world to his own mistaken misogyny:

> On my eyelids shall conjecture hang,
> To turn all beauty into thoughts of harm,
> And never shall it more be gracious. (IV.i.105–07)

Before he is forgiven and restored to his happiness, the Friar insists that the crime must be purged and punished in the place where it was committed—Claudio's own mind. Slander must change to remorse.

> Th' idea of her life shall sweetly creep
> Into his study of imagination, . . .
> Into the eye and prospect of his soul . . .
>   Then shall he mourn . . .
> And wish he had not so accused her.

The reconciliation scene is as melodramatic as the denunciation. It too plays with the paradoxes of true love that transcends, or runs counter to, this world of shadows. The resurrected Hero presents the truth as a conceit:

> And when I liv'd I was your other wife;
> And when you lov'd you were my other husband. (V.iv.60–61)

Leonato enforces love's transcendence: "She died, my lord, but whiles her slander liv'd." And the Friar reaffirms the joy and the remorse before the miraculous grace of love that will not die: "Meantime let wonder seem familiar."

The trouble is that in the main plot wonder does not seem familiar enough. The operatic situations and the ill-developed or poorly motivated characters are not convincing. Shakespeare rescues them through his favorites, Benedick and Beatrice. The denunciation scene turns from verse to prose, from melodrama to drama, when the stage is left to the two lovers and Benedick asks the question that shows again Shakespeare's dramatic use of silence: "Lady Beatrice, have you wept all this while?" She does not weep much longer, nor does she allow Benedick to fall into conventional vows of love. When he protests: "Bid me do anything for thee," she answers in two words: "Kill Claudio."[2] As she thinks of Claudio, her bitter eloquence pronounces a moral judgment not only on his blindness but on the unnecessary cruelty of his procedure:

> O that I were a man! What? bear her in hand until they come to take hands, and then with public accusation, uncover'd slander, unmitigated rancor—O God, that I were a man! I would eat his heart in the market place. (IV.i. 301–05)

Mere words are useless. When Benedick swears "By this hand, I love thee," Beatrice retorts: "Use it for my love some other way than swearing by it." And Benedick replies with equal economy: "Enough, I am engag'd, I will challenge him." Actions will speak, and "As you hear of me, so think of me." Benedick has had to choose between loyalty to Claudio and love for Beatrice. The greater love eclipses the smaller, and Benedick acts contrary to the presented evidence, on the strength of his trust in Beatrice's loyal love. Faith begets faith. He has asked but one question: "Think you *in your soul* the Count Claudio hath wrong'd her?" She answers: "Yea, as sure as I have a thought or a soul." And the debate in his mind has been decided in favor of Beatrice.

This is serious matter for comedy. But Shakespeare had long felt restive at the thought of mere manners passing for sound coin. In the court of love, there had been too much courtliness and courtesy, not enough love. This is evident in Berowne's renunciation of "taffeta phrases, silken terms precise," as well as in the portrayal of the villain Tybalt in *Romeo and Juliet* as one of "these antic,

---

[2] Another book on Shakespeare waiting to be written is *Shakespeare's Short Speeches*. Cf. Shylock's "I am content," and the many other examples, increasing as he learns his art, in which a short speech of not more than four words, usually monosyllables, marks a turn in the action or the highest dramatic point of a scene or of a whole play.

lisping, affecting fantasticoes—these new tuners of accent!" Portia herself waxes sarcastic against the tribe of immature swaggerers and the "thousand raw tricks of these bragging Jacks." And Beatrice showers vitriol on such courageous captains of compliment:

> But manhood is melted into cursies, valor into compliment, and men are only turn'd into tongue, and trim ones too. He is now as valiant as Hercules that only tells a lie, and swears it. (IV.i.316–20)

Old Antonio, uncle to Beatrice and Hero, grieving at the younger generation, carries on the tongue-lashing of these "Boys, apes, braggarts, Jacks, milksops!" "I know them," he says:

> I know them, yea,
> And what they weigh, even to the utmost scruple,
> Scambling, outfacing, fashionmonging boys,
> That lie and cog and flout, deprave and slander,
> Go anticly, show outward hideousness,
> And speak off half a dozen dang'rous words,
> How they might hurt their enemies, if they durst;
> And this is all. (V.i.92–99)

Why has Shakespeare taken such an antipathy to the vain young slanderers, the hotheaded lying Jacks of which Tybalt, and Claudio in *Much Ado,* show possible varieties? In part because he loathed particularly those evil elements that base their hostile actions on unfounded suspicion or on nothing whatever. Jealousy and slander he viewed with special aversion, for how can chastity and integrity oppose them? They mock our eyes with air. Of the two, slander may be the more sordid, since jealousy at least springs from misguided passion, whereas slander is purely malicious, destructive, and irresponsible. Who steals my purse steals trash; and outlaws are not such bad fellows, as *The Two Gentlemen of Verona* and *As You Like It* testify. But the slanderers, almost alone among Shakespeare's sinners, are nearly unforgivable; and Shakespeare, like Spenser, treats with revulsion the Bla-

tant Beast whose myriad tongues wound for sheer spite.
In the plays with political implications, of course, slander
becomes even more criminal than in the dramas of personal fortune.

Partly Shakespeare is bitter against the young swagger-
ing slanderers out of his usual contempt for pretension
in any form. And partly he seems to have developed, with
considerable deliberation, a distrust for the cocksureness
of callow youth. He works himself into a rather curious
position: the smooth, privileged young men are too young
to know what they are talking about; on the other hand,
old age with its wise saws is impotent in convincing any-
body. There seems little left for Shakespeare to acknowledge as a principle for conduct except Poor Richard's
adage, "Experience keeps a dear school, but fools will
learn in no other." Men's passions make all of them fools,
incapable of accepting any sage advice or profiting from
any hard-won experience except their own. Let us take
a formally developed illustration. When old Leonato is
grieving for his daughter Hero's shame, his yet older
brother Antonio admonishes him:

> If you go on thus, you will kill yourself,
> And 'tis not wisdom thus to second grief
> Against yourself. (V.i.1–3)

Leonato answers in a thirty-line speech, "I pray thee cease
thy counsel," the gist of which is that no one can console
him except a comforter "whose wrongs do suit with mine,"
that no man can patch his grief with a few proverbs, that
only those who do not feel grief mouth comfortable counsel, that aches cannot be charmed with air, nor agony
with words. He ends with certainty:

> No, no! 'Tis all men's office to speak patience
> To those that wring under the load of sorrow,
> But no man's virtue nor sufficiency
> To be so moral when he shall endure
> The like himself. Therefore give me no counsel.
> My griefs cry louder than advertisement.

And old brother Antonio answers with too much truth: "Therein do men from children nothing differ." Knowledge of this lamentable fact in human behavior is not the monopoly of the old men. Benedick has said earlier in the play: "Well, every one can master a grief but he that has it." And Romeo had answered the Friar's soothing wisdom in some irritation: "Thou canst not speak of that thou dost not feel."[3]

To sum it up, Shakespeare is no believer in the schoolroom. Copybook maxims, admirable as they may be, are ineffective. The only school is experience, and axioms are proved upon the pulses. Believing this, Shakespeare finds the drama a most excellent moral instrument, since in the drama characters reach conclusions by putting their various conflicting beliefs into action. Their passions and philosophies are forced to work out practicable solutions, in conflict with a larger world and with unsympathetic alien forces or personalities. The audience may profit vicariously from the display of life in action. This belief, so slowly affirmed, accounts for the greater soundness and sanity of Shakespeare's handling of love in the Golden Comedies. Romantic love, in the characters that interest him in *Much Ado About Nothing,* is not to be a doctrine promulgated to puppet lovers and forced upon them. Benedick and Beatrice will fight it to the last gasp. They take their stand against sentimentality, and carry on the war between the sexes with gusto.

The main interest of the play, then, starts in the world of common sense. Raillery and wit will protect light hearts. "There is measure in everything," says Beatrice, and lest that remark on moderation sound immoderately serious, she makes it into a pun and dances out her conviction. The lovers are too clear-eyed not to be self-critical. When Beatrice overhears her disdain, scornful wit, and self-endearment exaggerated, she abandons them. "Contempt,

---

[3] Shakespeare does not forget the ineffectiveness of sage advice. Compare Brabantio's bitter reply to the Duke of Venice (*Othello,* I.iii. 199–219) or Hamlet's attitude toward the sage counsel of Claudius (I.ii.87–120). See also Polonius and Laertes, the Duke of Vienna and Claudio, and the more knowing course of action Ulysses adopts toward both Achilles and Troilus.

farewell! and maiden pride, adieu!" And when Benedick also overhears a conversation on his character—that he will scorn Beatrice's love, since he "hath a contemptible spirit"—he decides to forsake "quips and sentences and these paper bullets of the brain," because, he says, "I must not seem proud. Happy are they that hear their detractions and can put them to mending." Part of this, of course, is not the result of the lovers' good resolutions, but of their instinctive attraction toward each other. "Good Lord, for alliance!" cries Beatrice, as she watches Claudio and Hero making love, and there is a touch of envy and self-pity in her jest: "Thus goes every one to the world but I. . . . I may sit in a corner and cry 'Heigh-ho for a husband!' "

"Alliance," then, catches these two independent spirits, who have too much good sense to resist nature. Leonato in his passion of grief had asserted:

> I will be flesh and blood;
> For there was never yet philosopher
> That could endure the toothache patiently.

Now Benedick feels the pangs of love, and when his friends twit him on his sadness, he replies: "I have the toothache." They ascribe it to love and suggest a remedy, but Benedick already knows well that "Yet is this no charm for the toothache."

To himself, he will not deny the effects and the power of love. Yet he will try to keep it in proportion through humor:

> Leander the good swimmer, Troilus the first employer of panders, and a whole book full of these quondam carpetmongers, whose names yet run smoothly in the even road of a blank verse—why, they were never so truly turn'd over and over as my poor self in love. (V.ii. 30–36)

He has too much respect for his genuine feelings to transform them into fashionable conventions; he "cannot woo in festival terms," and when he looks for rhymes for

Newsweek
Student Savings Voucher

Special offer also includes
FREE Newsweek On Campus subscription

NEWSWEEK'S COVER PRICE	$1.95
REGULAR SUBSCRIPTION PRICE	75¢
YOUR SPECIAL STUDENT PRICE	40¢

Name _____

Address _____

City _____ State _____ Zip _____

College _____ Year of Graduation _____

Signature _____

Check one:

☐ 26 issues ☐ 34 issues ☐ 52 issues ☐ 104 issues

☐ Payment enclosed ☐ Bill me later

*Newsweek On Campus is included as a supplement in Newsweek student subscription. Offer good in U.S. Subject to change.

ALMOST 80% OFF

Newsweek **OnCampus**
THE CONSERVATIVE STUDENT

Newsweek

CAMBODIA
Vietnam's Deadly Agony

Eddie Murphy
Mr. Box Office

852C4005

"lady," "scorn," and "school," he can only come out with "baby," "horn," and "fool." Sentiment—even when it is experienced directly—is to be kept in its place by anti-sentiment.

His sincerity is best shown in that excellently conceived dramatic scene of his challenge to Claudio. Here we have dramatic reversal of moods, for the perpetual giber Benedick is now in deadly earnest—"You have among you kill'd a sweet and innocent lady"—and his friends Pedro and Claudio are uneasily jesting against his estrangement and their own bad consciences. In critical moments Benedick controls both his emotion and his wit; their interaction protects him at once against the affectations of intellect and the extreme sallies of passion.

The integrity and sincerity of his love, based so broadly, make him in the end impervious to mockery, and it is "Benedick, the married man" who, after kissing Beatrice heartily, replies in all surety: "I'll tell thee what, Prince: a college of wit-crackers cannot flout me out of my humor," who demands music and dancing, and who advises Pedro: "Prince, thou art sad. Get thee a wife!" In the wedding of Benedick and Beatrice, humor has been married to love on both sides of the family. Since humor presupposes a greater consciousness of the world and of one's self, the wedding promises more stability and happiness than in any of Shakespeare's previous imaginings. "Man is a giddy thing," says Benedick, "and this is my conclusion." Man is less giddy, surer in his moral sense, in direct proportion to his awareness of his own giddiness.

W. H. AUDEN

from *The Dyer's Hand*

The called-for songs in *Much Ado About Nothing, As You Like It,* and *Twelfth Night* illustrate Shakespeare's skill in making what might have been beautiful irrelevancies contribute to the dramatic structure.

> *Much Ado About Nothing*
> Act II. Scene iii.
> *Song.* Sigh no more, ladies.
> *Audience. Don Pedro, Claudio, and Benedick (in hiding).*

In the two preceding scenes we have learned of two plots, Don Pedro's plot to make Benedick fall in love with Beatrice, and Don John's plot to make Claudio believe that Hero, his wife-to-be, is unchaste. Since this is a comedy, we, the audience, know that all will come right in the end, that Beatrice and Benedick, Claudio and Hero will get happily married.

The two plots of which we have just learned, therefore, arouse two different kinds of suspense. If the plot against Benedick succeeds, we are one step nearer the goal; if the plot against Claudio succeeds, we are one step back.

At this point, between their planning and their execu-

From *The Dyer's Hand and Other Essays* by W. H. Auden. New York: Random House, Inc., 1962; London: Faber & Faber, Ltd., 1963. © Copyright, 1957, by W. H. Auden. Reprinted by permission of the publishers.

tion, action is suspended, and we and the characters are made to listen to a song.

The scene opens with Benedick laughing at the thought of the lovesick Claudio and congratulating himself on being heart-whole, and he expresses their contrasted states in musical imagery.

> I have known him when there was no music with him but the drum and the fife; and now had he rather hear the tabor and the pipe. . . . Is it not strange that sheep's guts should hale souls out of men's bodies?—Well, a horn for my money, when all's done.

We, of course, know that Benedick is not as heart-whole as he is trying to pretend. Beatrice and Benedick resist each other because, being both proud and intelligent, they do not wish to be the helpless slaves of emotion or, worse, to become what they have often observed in others, the victims of an imaginary passion. Yet whatever he may say against music, Benedick does not go away, but stays and listens.

Claudio, for his part, wishes to hear music because he is in a dreamy, lovesick state, and one can guess that his *petit roman* as he listens will be of himself as the ever-faithful swain, so that he will not notice that the mood and words of the song are in complete contrast to his daydream. For the song is actually about the irresponsibility of men and the folly of women taking them seriously, and recommends as an antidote good humor and common sense. If one imagines these sentiments being the expression of a character, the only character they suit is Beatrice.

Leonato. . . . She is never sad but when she sleeps, and not ever sad then; for I have heard my daughter say she hath often dreamt of unhappiness and waked herself with laughing.

Don Pedro. She cannot endure to hear tell of a husband.

Leonato. O, by no means! She mocks all her wooers out of suit.

I do not think it too farfetched to imagine that the song

arouses in Benedick's mind an image of Beatrice, the tenderness of which alarms him. The violence of his comment when the song is over is suspicious:

> I pray God, his bad voice bode no mischief! I had as lief have heard the night-raven, come what plague could have come after it.

And, of course, there *is* mischief brewing. Almost immediately he overhears the planned conversation of Claudio and Don Pedro, and it has its intended effect. The song may not have compelled his capitulation, but it has certainly softened him up.

More mischief comes to Claudio who, two scenes later, shows himself all too willing to believe Don John's slander before he has been shown even false evidence, and declares that, if it should prove true, he will shame Hero in public. Had his love for Hero been all he imagined it to be, he would have laughed in Don John's face and believed Hero's assertion of her innocence, despite apparent evidence to the contrary, as immediately as her cousin does. He falls into the trap set for him because as yet he is less a lover than a man in love with love. Hero is as yet more an image in his own mind than a real person, and such images are susceptible to every suggestion.

For Claudio, the song marks the moment when his pleasant illusions about himself as a lover are at their highest. Before he can really listen to music he must be cured of imaginary listening, and the cure lies through the disharmonious experiences of passion and guilt.

Suggested References

The number of possible references is vast and grows alarmingly. (The *Shakespeare Quarterly* devotes a substantial part of one issue each year to a list of the previous year's work, and *Shakespeare Survey*—an annual publication—includes a substantial review of recent scholarship, as well as an occasional essay surveying a few decades of scholarship on a chosen topic.) Though no works are indispensable, those listed below have been found helpful.

1. Shakespeare's Times

Byrne, M. St. Clare. *Elizabethan Life in Town and Country*. Rev. ed. New York: Barnes & Noble, Inc., 1961. Chapters on manners, beliefs, education, etc., with illustrations.

Craig, Hardin. *The Enchanted Glass: the Elizabethan Mind in Literature*. New York and London: Oxford University Press, 1936. The Elizabethan intellectual climate.

Joseph, B. L. *Shakespeare's Eden: The Commonwealth of England 1558–1629*. New York: Barnes & Noble, Inc., 1971. An account of the social, political, economic, and cultural life of England.

Nicoll, Allardyce (ed.). *The Elizabethans*. London: Cambridge University Press, 1957. An anthology of Elizabethan writings, especially valuable for its illustrations from paintings, title pages, etc.

Shakespeare's England. 2 vols. Oxford: The Clarendon Press, 1916. A large collection of scholarly essays on a wide variety of topics (e.g., astrology, costume, gardening, horsemanship), with special attention to Shakespeare's references to these topics.

Tillyard, E. M. W. *The Elizabethan World Picture*. London: Chatto & Windus, 1943; New York: The Macmillan Company, 1944. A brief account of some Elizabethan ideas of the universe.

Wilson, John Dover (ed.). *Life in Shakespeare's England*. 2nd ed. New York: The Macmillan Company, 1913. An anthology of Elizabethan writings on the countryside, superstition, education, the court, etc.

2. Shakespeare

Barnet, Sylvan. *A Short Guide to Shakespeare*. New York: Harcourt Brace Jovanovich, Inc., 1974. An introduction to all of the works and to the traditions behind them.

Bentley, Gerald E. *Shakespeare: A Biographical Handbook*. New Haven, Conn.: Yale University Press, 1961. The facts about Shakespeare, with virtually no conjecture intermingled.

Bradby, Anne (ed.). *Shakespeare Criticism, 1919–1935*. London: Oxford University Press, 1936. A small anthology of excellent essays on the plays.

Bush, Geoffrey Douglas. *Shakespeare and the Natural Condition*. Cambridge, Mass.: Harvard University Press; London: Oxford University Press, 1956. A short, sensitive account of Shakespeare's view of "Nature," touching most of the works.

Chambers, E. K. *William Shakespeare: A Study of Facts and Problems*. 2 vols. London: Oxford University Press, 1930. An invaluable, detailed reference work; not for the casual reader.

Chute, Marchette. *Shakespeare of London*. New York: E. P. Dutton & Co., Inc., 1949. A readable biography fused with portraits of Stratford and London life.

Clemen, Wolfgang H. *The Development of Shakespeare's Imagery*. Cambridge, Mass.: Harvard University Press, 1951. (Originally published in German, 1936.) A temperate account of a subject often abused.

Craig, Hardin. *An Interpretation of Shakespeare*. Columbia, Missouri: Lucas Brothers, 1948. A scholar's book designed for the layman. Comments on all the works.

Dean, Leonard F. (ed.). *Shakespeare: Modern Essays in Criticism*. New York: Oxford University Press, 1957. Mostly mid-twentieth-century critical studies, covering Shakespeare's artistry.

Granville-Barker, Harley. *Prefaces to Shakespeare*. 2 vols. Princeton, N.J.: Princeton University Press, 1946–47. Essays on ten plays by a scholarly man of the theater.

Harbage, Alfred. *As They Liked It*. New York: The Macmillan Company, 1947. A sensitive, long essay on Shakespeare, morality, and the audience's expectations.

————. *William Shakespeare: A Reader's Guide*. New York: Farrar, Straus, 1963. Extensive comments, scene by scene, on fourteen plays.

Ridler, Anne Bradby (ed.). *Shakespeare Criticism, 1935–1960*. New York and London: Oxford University Press, 1963. An excellent continuation of the anthology edited earlier by Miss Bradby (see above).

Schoenbaum, S. *Shakespeare's Lives*. Oxford: Clarendon Press, 1970. A review of the evidence, and an examination of many biographies, including those by Baconians and others.

————. *William Shakespeare: A Compact Documentary Life*. New York: Oxford University Press, 1977. A readable presentation of all that the documents tell us about Shakespeare.

Smith, D. Nichol (ed.). *Shakespeare Criticism*. New York: Oxford University Press, 1916. A selection of criticism from 1623 to 1840, ranging from Ben Jonson to Thomas Carlyle.

Spencer, Theodore. *Shakespeare and the Nature of Man*. New York: The Macmillan Company, 1942. Shakespeare's plays in relation to Elizabethan thought.

Stoll, Elmer Edgar. *Shakespeare and Other Masters*. Cambridge, Mass.: Harvard University Press; London: Oxford University Press, 1940. Essays on tragedy, comedy, and aspects of dramaturgy, with special reference to some of Shakespeare's plays.

Traversi, D. A. *An Approach to Shakespeare*. Rev. ed. New York: Doubleday & Co., Inc., 1956. An analysis of the plays, beginning with words, images, and themes, rather than with characters.

Van Doren, Mark. *Shakespeare*. New York: Henry Holt & Company, Inc., 1939. Brief, perceptive readings of all of the plays.

Whitaker, Virgil K. *Shakespeare's Use of Learning*. San Marino, Calif.: Huntington Library, 1953. A study of the relation of Shakespeare's reading to his development as a dramatist.

3. Shakespeare's Theater

Adams, John Cranford. *The Globe Playhouse*. Rev. ed. New York: Barnes & Noble, Inc., 1961. A detailed conjecture about the physical characteristics of the theater Shakespeare often wrote for.

Beckerman, Bernard. *Shakespeare at the Globe, 1599–1609*. New York: The Macmillan Company, 1962. On the playhouse and on Elizabethan dramaturgy, acting, and staging.

Chambers, E. K. *The Elizabethan Stage.* 4 vols. New York: Oxford University Press, 1923. Reprinted with corrections, 1945. An indispensable reference work on theaters, theatrical companies, and staging at court.

Gurr, Andrew. *The Shakespearean Stage 1574–1642.* Cambridge: Cambridge University Press, 1970. On the acting companies, the actors, the playhouses, the stages, and the audiences.

Harbage, Alfred. *Shakespeare's Audience.* New York: Columbia University Press; London: Oxford University Press, 1941. A study of the size and nature of the theatrical public.

Hodges, C. Walter. *The Globe Restored.* London: Ernest Benn, Ltd., 1953; New York: Coward-McCann, Inc., 1954. A well-illustrated and readable attempt to reconstruct the Globe Theatre.

Kernodle, George R. *From Art to Theatre: Form and Convention in the Renaissance.* Chicago: University of Chicago Press, 1944. Pioneering and stimulating work on the symbolic and cultural meanings of theater construction.

Nagler, A. M. *Shakespeare's Stage.* Tr. by Ralph Manheim. New Haven, Conn.: Yale University Press, 1958. An excellent brief introduction to the physical aspect of the playhouse.

Smith, Irwin. *Shakespeare's Globe Playhouse.* New York: Charles Scribner's Sons, 1957. Chiefly indebted to J. C. Adams' controversial book, with additional material and scale drawings for model-builders.

Venezky, Alice S. *Pageantry on the Shakespearean Stage.* New York: Twayne Publishers, Inc., 1951. An examination of spectacle in Elizabethan drama.

4. Miscellaneous Reference Works

Abbott, E. A. *A Shakespearean Grammar.* New edition. New York: The Macmillan Company, 1877. An examination of differences between Elizabethan and modern grammar.

Bullough, Geoffrey. *Narrative and Dramatic Sources of Shakespeare.* 4 vols. Vols. 5 and 6 in preparation. New York: Columbia University Press; London: Routledge & Kegan Paul, Ltd. 1957–. A collection of many of the books Shakespeare drew upon.

Campbell, Oscar James, and Edward G. Quinn. *The Reader's Encyclopedia of Shakespeare.* New York: Thomas Y. Crowell Co., 1966. More than 2,700 entries, from a few sentences to a few pages on everything related to Shakespeare.

Greg, W. W. *The Shakespeare First Folio.* New York and London: Oxford University Press, 1955. A detailed yet readable history of the first collection (1623) of Shakespeare's plays.

Kökeritz, Helge. *Shakespeare's Names.* New Haven, Conn.: Yale University Press, 1959; London: Oxford University Press, 1960. A guide to the pronunciation of some 1,800 names appearing in Shakespeare.

———. *Shakespeare's Pronunciation.* New Haven, Conn.: Yale University Press; London: Oxford University Press, 1953. Contains much information about puns and rhymes.

Linthicum, Marie C. *Costume in the Drama of Shakespeare and His Contemporaries.* New York and London: Oxford University Press, 1936. On the fabrics and dress of the age, and references to them in the plays.

Muir, Kenneth. *Shakespeare's Sources.* London: Methuen & Co., Ltd., 1957. The first volume, on the comedies and tragedies, attempts to ascertain what books were Shakespeare's sources, and what use he made of them.

Onions, C. T. *A Shakespeare Glossary.* London: Oxford University Press, 1911; 2nd ed., rev., with enlarged addenda, 1953. Definitions of words (or senses of words) now obsolete.

Partridge, Eric. *Shakespeare's Bawdy.* Rev. ed. New York: E. P. Dutton & Co., Inc.; London: Routledge & Kegan Paul, Ltd., 1955. A glossary of bawdy words and phrases.

Shakespeare Quarterly. See headnote to Suggested References.

Shakespeare Survey. See headnote to Suggested References.

Smith, Gordon Ross. *A Classified Shakespeare Bibliography, 1936–1958.* University Park, Pa.: Pennsylvania State University Press, 1963. A list of some 20,000 items on Shakespeare.

Spevack, Marvin. *The Harvard Concordance to Shakespeare.* Cambridge, Mass.: Harvard University Press, 1973. An index to Shakespeare's words.

Wells, Stanley, ed. *Shakespeare: Select Bibliographies.* London: Oxford University Press, 1973. Seventeen essays surveying scholarship and criticism of Shakespeare's life, work, and theater.

5. Much Ado About Nothing

Craik, T. W. "*Much Ado About Nothing,*" *Scrutiny,* 19 (1953), 297–316.

Davis, Walter R., ed. *Twentieth Century Interpretations of "Much Ado About Nothing."* Englewood Cliffs, New Jersey: Prentice-Hall, Inc., 1969.

Evans, Bertrand. *Shakespeare's Comedies.* New York and London: Oxford University Press, 1960.

Everett, Barbara. "*Much Ado About Nothing,*" *Critical Quarterly,* 3 (1961), 319–35.

Jorgensen, Paul A. "*Much Ado About Nothing,*" *Shakespeare Quarterly,* 5 (1954), 287–95.

Leggatt, Alexander. *Shakespeare's Comedy of Love.* London: Methuen & Co., 1974.

Lewalski, B. K. "Love, Appearance and Reality: Much Ado about Something," *Studies in English Literature,* 8 (1968), 235–51.

Mulryne, J. R. *Shakespeare: "Much Ado about Nothing."* London: Edward Arnold Ltd., 1965.

Neill, Kirby. "More Ado About Claudio: An Acquittal for the Slandered Groom," *Shakespeare Quarterly,* 3 (1952), 91–107.

Page, Nadine. "The Public Repudiation of Hero," *Publications of the Modern Language Association,* 50 (1935), 739–44.

Prouty, Charles T. *The Sources of "Much Ado About Nothing."* New Haven: Yale University Press, 1950; London: Oxford University Press, 1951.

Rossiter, A. P. "*Angel with Horns*" *and Other Shakespeare Lectures,* ed. Graham Storey. New York: Theatre Arts Books; London: Longmans, Green & Co., Ltd., 1961.

Stevenson, David L. *The Love-Game Comedy.* New York: Columbia University Press; London: Oxford University Press, 1946.

Stoll, Elmer Edgar. *Shakespeare's Young Lovers.* New York and London: Oxford University Press, 1937.

Storey, Graham. "The Success of *Much Ado About Nothing,*" *More Talking of Shakespeare,* ed. John Garrett. New York: Theatre Arts Books; London: Longmans, Green & Co., Ltd., 1959.